THE ESCORT NEXT DOOR

CAPTIVATED

Copyright © 2013 by Clara James

This is a work of fiction. Names, characters, places, and incidents either are the product of the author's imagination or are used fictitiously, and any resemblance to any persons, living or dead, business establishments, events, or locales is entirely coincidental.

The Escort Next: Door Captivated

All rights reserved.

This book is protected under the copyright laws of the United States of America. No part of this work may be used, reproduced, or transmitted in any form or by any means, electronic or mechanical, including photocopying, recording and faxing, or by any information storage and retrieval system by anyone but the purchaser for their own personal use.

This book may not be reproduced in any form without the express written permission of Clara James, except in the case of a reviewer who wishes to quote brief passages for the sake of a review written for inclusions in a magazine, newspaper, or journal—and these cases require written approval from Clara James prior to publication. Any reproduction or other unauthorized use of the material or artwork herein is prohibited without the express written permission of the author.

Fonts used with permission from Microsoft

Also by bestselling author

Clara James

~The Escort Next Door Series~

The Escort Next Door

The Escort Next Door: Captivated

The Escort Next Door: Escape

~Her Last Love Affair Series~

Her Last Love Affair

Her Last Love Affair: Breathing Without You

Her Last Love Affair: The Final Journey

To view these titles visit:
http://amzn.to/15ek5q7

PROLOGUE

Julia Hayes thought she'd married the perfect man; her high school sweetheart, the only guy she'd ever loved. The pair married young and within two years, Julia had given birth to their first child. Eight years and another two children later, Julia's husband has been made CEO of the successful family business.

The couple now seems to have everything; a beautiful little family, dream home and absolutely no financial worries. However, Julia had started to notice a change in Paul, something she initially put down to the long hours and extra stress of taking his father's place as head of the company. But what she believed was just a phase dragged on into weeks and, eventually, months.

Then, during one of his frequent business trips, she found something that explained his coldness and disinterest in intimacy: an empty condom wrapper. Desperate to find out what had been going on, she searched his things and discovered that he hadn't just been having one affair. For several months, he'd been having a string of one-night stands every time he went out of town.

Devastated, Julia determines to leave him. But before she's able to pack a bag, she realizes there's a problem. She has no job, no money of her own; she'd been a stay-at-home mom ever since their firstborn had arrived. Worse still, she'd signed a prenuptial agreement that ensures she gets nothing if she and Paul divorce. With three children to support, she was trapped. That is until her best friend proposed an interesting suggestion: stripping.

Exotic dancers can make a lot of money, in a relatively short time. Against her better judgment, Julia seriously begins to consider this is an option. However, she's forced to abandon the idea when she realizes her chances of getting caught are too high. Soon, a new idea surfaces. The clients of escorts are much more discreet than men who frequent strip clubs, and she could earn at least double what she would have done dancing.

It seems like the perfect solution. The only drawback was the thought of selling her body to strange men. Until the night with her first client, Julia had never slept with anyone other than her husband. She was nervous, petrified, in fact. But, as she begins to lose herself in the role, she learns there is a side of her that she hadn't ever really explored; a sluttish and sensual side.

With her first $2,000, she goes home and is already eagerly anticipating her next 'date'.

Chapter One
Pretend

When Paul arrived home later that afternoon, it was difficult to look at him. The images of him with that blonde girl loomed heavily in my brain, and my imagination was fertile in picturing what he'd been up to on his latest trip. The only thing that stopped me from clawing the walls was the knowledge of what I had done in turn.

I would not have dreamed of being unfaithful to him before. But 'before' seemed like another lifetime ago. He was different, I was different. Everything had changed.

As I made dinner, he drifted into the kitchen, picking up a raw chunk of carrot and chewing on it noisily. "Kids said they spent last night at my parents," he noted, his words muffled with the crunching.

"Yeah," I replied, casually. "Your mom thought I was having a tough time coping, didn't think I was keeping the house in order." I didn't bother to look at him as I spoke; my head was dipped to the sink, my gaze focused on the potatoes I was peeling. What I'd told him was the truth. Carole had been only too happy when I called and admitted I needed help. Of course, she gloated for the better part of thirty minutes, but that was a small price to pay.

"Oh, right," he said disinterestedly. "So, you spent the night cleaning?" It was spoken skeptically and I could see out of the corner of my eye that he was glancing around the large open plan kitchen and dining area.

Carefully placing the knife down on the edge of the sink, I lifted the bowl of peelings and slid it on the counter. "The children have been back for six hours," I explained, shrugging. "Trying to keep a home clean with three under ten year olds, is like brushing your teeth at the same time as eating an Oreo," I informed him, swiping at the bangs that were getting a little too long and falling into my eyes. "You should try it sometime," I added a little tartly, flashing a sarcastic smile at him.

"Are you still mad at me?" he said, not looking at me but focusing on his finger as he drew invisible circles on the granite island in the middle of the room.

I realized as he did that that he looked just like Dylan. Our son hadn't copied him, because Paul didn't use to behave evasively and sulkily like that. No, he'd regressed since our children came into the world.

"What?" I sighed, still focusing on my task.

"You've been..." he hovered over the words, waiting for another to come. "You've been different," he mumbled, "since I got back."

"I don't know what you mean," I breezily replied, reaching up to open a cupboard.

"You're usually happier to see me," he responded, still moodily staring at his hand.

Rolling my eyes, I grabbed the gravy powder and placed it on the counter. "I am happy to see you," I told him flatly, realizing when the sound hit my ears that it was probably the least convincing thing I'd ever said. "I'm just busy."

"So, you're not mad?"

"About what?" I sighed.

He was quiet for a few moments, as his finger circles grew smaller and faster. "The other night," he eventually murmured, glancing over his shoulder to ensure our little ones weren't in hearing distance.

Abandoning dinner for a minute, I turned to face him. Leaning the small of my back against the counter top, I studied his face. So he did have some conscience. It might have been infinitely small, but it was there. He did know the way he'd treated me was wrong, he did remember using my body with a complete disregard for the fact he was hurting me. "I thought you said it was no big deal," I pointed out, my arms reflexively crossing beneath my breasts.

"Well," he hedged, his eyes nervously moving everywhere in the room but on me. "I didn't mean-" he abruptly cut himself off, before taking a breath and a different tack. "I've had some time to think and I was selfish, it shouldn't have been all about me."

I wanted so badly to tell him that all evidence suggested the contrary. I wanted to ask him whether the many women he'd fucked during his business trips had found him selfish, too. However, I bit my tongue. I had to keep that knowledge to myself. If he realized what I knew, things would get even more complicated than they already were. No, I had to remain quiet and patient. I would get my revenge on him, eventually. It would just take some time. I could be patient, I had three children.

"Jules," he muttered, the shortening of my name was something he hadn't done for years. "Say something."

"It's fine," I said, almost choking on the words. It was far from 'fine'. "Like you said, it was no big deal. And maybe I've been putting too much pressure on you," I conceded, turning my back to him again, as it became increasingly harder to lie. "I don't mean to smother you; you're busy, you need time to unwind. I've been expecting romance and affection and it's just not realistic, is it?" I continued to speak as I grabbed a pan and placed it on the stove. "So, I've made a decision to give you some space," I explained, hoping that would both suit him and answer his question about why I was behaving differently. "Now," I sighed, tossing my head quickly over my shoulder. "You promised the children you'd spend some time with them," I reminded him.

He waited for a moment, his head gently rocking to one side. He looked like he was about to argue, to ask another question. However, he must have thought better of it. "All right," he said, smiling. "Shout when dinner's ready," he added, as he left the room.

For a moment, my fingers were still. If only I'd known that the way to get him to treat me better was to be a little frosty toward him. The old mantra, treat 'em mean, keep 'em keen, may actually have some truth to it. But perhaps it was fortunate I hadn't known that before. If everything had been peachy between us, I wouldn't have found out what he was doing and would be obliviously drifting through life. No, as painful as it all was, it was much better to know.

Later that evening, I remained pretty quiet as we ate; reflecting on how much the children loved their dad. Of course, they were all still at that age when you believe your father is the most amazing man in the world. They'd yet to discover that he was human; flawed and not in fact invincible. Still, it was going to be hard to take them away from him. How would I explain it to them? Would they grow up hating me for it? It was all too much to comprehend at that moment, besides I had so many other hurdles still to leap. My escape from Paul was far from a done deal.

I deliberately stayed up, professing a desire to want to watch something on TV, when Paul suggested it was time for bed. "You go ahead," I urged. "I'll be up in a little while."

Uncharacteristically, this seemed to bother him. Obviously our chat in the kitchen had done little to allay his fears that something was wrong. It occurred to me that I would have to be much more careful; I had to go back to behaving as I had before, because if I didn't, he was going to start getting suspicious.

"You're not tired?" he asked, standing by the end of the couch with his hand rested on the back.

"Not as much as I thought I'd be," I hummed thoughtfully. "I've been having a hard time getting to sleep these last few nights."

"Really?" he muttered, concern creasing his brow.

"It's nothing to worry about," I said with a wave of my hand. "Just one of those things." Reminding myself to act 'normally', I lifted my butt from the couch and kissed him gently on the lips. "Really, it's fine. I'll be up in a bit."

That seemed to appease him somewhat. "All right," he sighed, before yawning. With a quick bend at the waist, he placed his lips to the crown of my head.

Without another word, he turned and began to walk up the stairs. That was more like it; that was what 'normal' had become for us.

I didn't settle down to watch the TV, though. Instead, I leaned forward and grabbed my phone from the coffee table. With a few quick tips, I logged into the email address I'd set up specifically for communicating with potential clients. One message was from David, the man I'd seen the night before; my very first client. He thanked me for a great night and reminded me once more about his offer to pay for me to travel across the country and meet him wherever he happened to be working.

I was so tempted to take him up on it. He was a nice guy and, I had to admit, I was very attracted to him. So much so, I would have been prepared to see him again free of charge. Nevertheless, I couldn't risk taking a long trip. If the kids stayed with someone for longer than a night, Paul would wonder what was going on. No, I had to think of the bigger picture. So, I wrote back to David, telling him that I had an amazing time and that I appreciated his offer, but could not accept. I added that if ever he was in the state again, I would be more than happy to hear from him.

With a slightly sad sigh, I closed his email and scrolled down. Lower, I found three new emails. One was spam, but the other two seemed interesting. The first was from a man who called himself John. He lived a couple of towns over and said that he'd hired a couple of escorts in the past, but was looking for someone new. He asked me to meet him at a hotel the following Friday. The second email was from Steven, who told me he was an investment banker. Apparently, he was in the state for a job interview, and wanted some help relaxing the night before the big day. He wrote that he would not arrive for another couple of weeks; the 19th to be exact.

Jumping to my feet, I kept a tight hold of my phone as I wandered into the kitchen. Next to the fridge was a calendar, which my eyes quickly scanned. Paul was due to go away again on the 18th. He wasn't getting back until the 23rd. Steven's visit would fit perfectly within that timeframe.

I quickly wrote back, telling him that the date was good for me. While I was there, I replied to John, expressing my regret that I could not make the date that he wanted and asking if he would be interested in meeting a little later in the month.

Before I went to bed that night, I had two dates arranged for Paul's next trip. This time, rather than dreading him going away again, I was excited. Steven and John might not be able to live up to the very high standard set by my first encounter; but I was no longer worried about being able to 'perform' with a stranger. If all else failed, I had the memory of David going down on me. That mental image would be good for all kinds of scenarios.

Besides, I silently told myself, as I jogged up the stairs; I was quickly learning that there was an inner slut in me; a woman who loved sex and was excited by the prospect of it with strangers. Getting through my dates with those two men was not going to be the problem. It was getting through the next two weeks that would be hard.

Chapter Two

Kinky

Flutters of excitement became more and more pronounced as the day of my date with Steven drew closer. Like David, he asked to meet in a hotel. Although his interview was local to the area, he wanted to travel some distance for the sake of privacy and discretion. All of this was fine with me, and understandable.

As he'd asked, when I got to the hotel, I made my way to the bar. Perching on one of the high stools, I ordered a martini and tried to affect a demeanor of cool. My real emotions were quite the contrary; jittery, nervous, anxious and just a little bit aroused. Nevertheless, I calmly sipped on my cocktail, people watched, and waited for Steven to introduce himself.

What I didn't know at the time was that Steven was already in the room. He'd been there since I arrived, and had also been watching and waiting. It was five minutes before he made his move and, as he approached me, I assumed he was just some guy looking to chat me up.

I noticed him out of the corner of my eye; a middle-aged man, who must have been edging on fifty. He still had some color to his hair, but most of the brown had succumbed to the growing wealth of gray. It's silly to say, but it made him look more distinguished somehow. He was trim, obviously liked to stay fit, and was dressed quite casually; a dark pair of jeans and a pale blue polo shirt.

"Hey," he said, his voice a low, confident rumble. "How are you?"

"Umm," I hummed, tossing a glance over my shoulder. "I'm fine, thanks," I said, my face slowly moving back to him. "How are you?" I added through nothing more than politeness.

"I'm great," he said, smiling and showing me a healthy set of bright, white teeth. "Are you waiting for someone?" he asked.

"Yes, actually," I replied, nodding. "A friend," I explained.

"Oh," he nodded his understanding. "Well, that's nice," he mentioned, the smile growing broader. "I'm glad that you consider us friends already."

"Excuse me?" I muttered, believing I must have misheard him.

Rather than respond right away, he reached his hand out to me. "I'm Steven," he explained.

"Oh," I chuckled, "right." I continued to laugh lightly as I took his hand and gave it a brief shake. He wasn't aware of it, but I carefully monitored the way he grasped my fingers; not too tightly, but quite firm. His hand was mostly soft, but the fingers were a bit coarse, leading me to wonder what he did for that to be the case. However, it was not my place to ask. If he wanted to talk about his job or his hobbies, fine. But I'd realized it wasn't right to bring that, or anything else up, until the client did.

"Arianna, you are even more beautiful that in your picture," he commented.

"Well, thank you," I smiled, not finding myself quite as embarrassed as I had been when David called me 'beautiful'. Although it's terrible to say, I think the reason I didn't feel as awkward with Steven is that I didn't find him as attractive. He was a perfectly handsome man, but that special something; that chemistry that is either there or not, just wasn't present with him. And while that chemistry was definitely helpful during my first job, it had also proven to be something of a stumbling block. It was much harder getting into the 'role' of an escort, when

I was so taken aback by the magnetism I felt for David.

This time, I thought to myself, things would be different; and maybe they'd be better, because I wouldn't feel so clumsily bashful every time Steven spoke to me.

"Can I sit down?" he suggested, gesturing to the bar stool next to me. It was strange the way he behaved, as if he'd just met me, as if this wasn't all staged and it would actually be very peculiar if my answer was 'no'. But if he wanted to pretend, that was fine by me. The whole date was a pretense, after all.

"Sure," I smiled, tipping my head towards the seat.

Two days earlier, Steven had sent a brief email asking me to have a certain 'look' on the night itself. So, following his instructions, I was dressed in a simple, black shift dress, with my hair up in a French twist. My fingernails and toes were painted a deep shade of red, and I wore a lipstick that matched it. It was clear to me that Steven had very specific ideas about what he wanted the night to be. In a way, that was helpful. If an escort knows what a man wants her to be, then it's far easier for her to play the role. It's when she doesn't really know what turns him on, that she's forced to think on her feet and play by ear.

The Escort Next Door

As Steven sat at the bar, he stretched his left hand out on the counter top in front of him. He was wearing a simple gold band on his ring finger; the only piece of jewelry, other than a watch, that he had on.

For a moment, I froze. This was not exactly a revelation; I'd realized that plenty of men who hire escorts have wives and children. Yet I'd made the mistake of assuming they hide it. What I didn't know about, I could assume didn't exist. I know it was silly, burying my head in the sand didn't change anything. But somehow, knowing that Steven had a wife; knowing that she was just like I had been, oblivious to my husband's affairs, left a very bad taste in my mouth.

I guess the change in my expression and the direction of my eyes didn't go unnoticed by him, because he soon slipped his hand back and hastened it into his pocket. "It's not what you think," he mumbled.

I tried to give him a naïve look to suggest I didn't know what he was referring to.

"I'll explain," he assured me, with a confident nod. "It's...umm," he added, before pausing. "Well, it's not as bad as it looks."

"It's absolutely none of my business," I said, taking a sip of my drink. "You don't owe me an explanation."

"Maybe not," he accepted. "But I'd like to give you one anyway."

I shrugged, indicating that it was up to him what he told me and how much. "I'm just here to enjoy your company," I added, focusing on the job at hand and sweeping all other thoughts from my mind. It wasn't my responsibility, I silently told myself. I can feel sorry for his wife, but it's not going to alter the fact that he's cheated; probably many times – he definitely seems familiar with the process of hiring a call girl. I wasn't the first and would not be the last.

We shared a couple of drinks, and moved the conversation onto less problematic topics; the weather, his love of golf, the kind of music he liked and the literature he enjoys. It was comfortable, it was easy. And as we talked, I was careful not to drink too quickly. Getting tipsy the first time was understandable, but now I had to learn to do this without the crutch of alcohol. Otherwise, I was heading for a world of trouble; not least the hangovers that would haunt me the next morning.

It was about an hour until he smoothly suggested we move the chat upstairs to his room. The bartender must have overheard, but he didn't bat an eye. I did, however, notice the stare of a couple of women who'd been sitting in the corner of the room. They were my age, perhaps a little older and had been tossing glances at me and Steven the entire time. Maybe they guessed what I was, or maybe they thought I was just a slut. Either way, the pair of them flashed me a dirty look.

As we passed them, I smiled and looped my arm through Steven's. I was beyond caring what people thought. They had no right to judge me; no one has the right to judge until they've been trapped in a situation with only one way out. We all have a price, don't we? My price isn't what I charge per hour. My 'price' is the ability to leave my husband and keep my children with me. For that, I would sell anything.

Steven, meanwhile, led me to the elevator and pushed the circular silver button to call the car. "I think those women were jealous of how hot you look," he commented casually.

I hadn't even realized he'd noticed them, much less seen the look they tossed their eyes our way. Looking up into his gaze, I smiled gratefully. "Perhaps they were jealous that I was with you," I retorted, with a sultry voice and a saucy grin. It was all about making the client feel good, and, who knows, maybe those women did think I'd landed a silver fox. He was a handsome guy, with a George Clooney-like charm. Now, George Clooney might not have rung my bell, but that doesn't mean I can't appreciate a well put together man when I see one. And there were many, many women who would kill to be with old George.

Clara James

As he smiled, a little wider than he had all night, I saw that one of his back teeth was gold. With all of the others in such great condition, I found it hard to believe it fell out or was removed for health reasons. It was a silly thing to wonder about, but wonder I did. Was there a good story behind that tooth? Because I had such a short space of time to get to know him, it was the little things that I was drawn to.

"Come on," he encouraged, as the elevator doors slid open.

Unhooking my arm from his, he placed his hand on the small of my back, gently guiding me into the car. "Are we going far?" I asked, making small talk with a deliberate double entendre to it. It wasn't overt, it wasn't said with a nudge and a wink – if he construed anything sexual, it was him and not me that had done so. It was subtle and, I hoped, classy.

The mischievous quirk of his lips told me exactly where his mind had gone. He didn't say anything; he didn't need to.

We traveled to the sixth floor and he chivalrously insisted that I exit the elevate car first. Then, we walked in step toward his room. Conversation had dried up, but it wasn't an uncomfortable silence; on the contrary, it was the kind of quiet that descends when words simply aren't necessary.

The Escort Next Door

I'd assumed they would be even less necessary when we got into the room. However, as he carefully closed the door and invited me to sit, he apparently had other ideas about what was and wasn't needed.

"Now," he sighed, watching me lower myself into an armchair, while he perched on the edge of the bed. "About..." he left the word hanging, lifting his left hand and indicating his wedding ring.

"I meant what I said," I told him, smiling. "It really hasn't got anything to do with me."

"That might very well be true," he nodded, lowering his hand. Pressing both together, he slipped his hands between his slightly parted knees. "But I want you to know that I love my wife."

It seemed like such an incongruous thing to utter that I was speechless. The me of a month or more ago wouldn't have been able to hold back the thought that was rolling through my head: 'You can't possibly love your wife and want to sleep with other women'. The new me was quicker to bite her tongue, but not just because she was being paid to do so. The lines between right and wrong were becoming a little blurry.

"I adore me wife," he added with emphasis. "We're good together; she's my best friend and the mother of my children. She's everything to me."

The more he talked, the more confused I was. Did men who have affairs make a habit of talking so affectionately about the women they're being unfaithful to? I think my look of complete confusion must have been evident.

Steven chuckled, dipping his chin toward his chest. "I know that this seems completely contrary to that statement," he conceded, gesturing between himself and me on the word 'this'. "But she knows about this," he stated, as if it were the most natural and obvious thing in the world. "I mean," he added, shaking his head. "She doesn't know exactly about this, but she knows that I occasionally..." He paused, his hand lifting from its constrained spot between his legs and gesturing in a feeble rolling motion.

"Use escorts?" I supplied for him.

"Yeah," he responded gratefully. "She knows that I sometimes hire the services of women like you."

"Umm, okay," I nodded, unsure why it was important to him that I know this and how he expected it to put either of us in the mood. Was it a turn on for him?

"She's not thrilled by it," he added with a rueful smile. "But she accepts it, because I have...Well, I have particular needs."

"Oh, I see," I replied with a calmness I didn't feel. I had no idea what he meant by 'needs'. After being so specific about how he wanted me to dress and where he wanted me to meet him, it seemed strange that he wouldn't mention a particular preference he had. Did that mean it was something indecent? His wife obviously thought so.

Nervously rubbing at his upper lip with the pad of one finger, he seemed to think carefully about his next words. "I probably should have mentioned when I first contacted you," he admitted. "But I was hoping...I was hoping that it wouldn't be a problem."

"Well, I'm sure it won't be," I smiled, praying that I looked much more at ease than I felt.

"Good," he beamed, that gold tooth showing once more. "Good," he repeated. "You see I'm into...umm..." he faltered. "Bondage," he eventually stated. "Humiliation," he added.

"Okay," I nodded, remaining calm. BDSM wasn't an uncommon fantasy. As soon as I'd decided to become an escort, I'd made a point of reading as much as I could about the most popular male sexual tastes, and that was right up there. Having initially known very little about it, I researched some of the basics in case of just such a situation. Of course, I still didn't exactly know what Steven wanted to do with me: tie me up, spank me, blindfold me, gag me, torture me maybe? If his wife was so opposed to it, then it must have been something beyond the light, playful BDSM lots of couples enjoyed together.

"That's great," he said, getting to his feet. "I'm really pleased, you feel that way" he added. "Because I knew, the moment I saw you, that I wanted you to dominate me."

Chapter Three

Mistress

At first, I thought I must have misheard him. After a few moments, I wondered if I'd misunderstood. However, neither of those things had happened – and deep down I knew it. I gasped at the possibilities though, because I knew I was in over my head.

I'd mentally prepared myself for the kind of things I might be subjected to as a submissive partner. Taking control of the scenario in order to play a dominant role was, perhaps stupidly, not something I'd considered. And I was certain it was not in my nature to be dominant, especially not sexually.

"If you'd like to come into the bathroom," he offered as he moved to the door and pushed it open. "I've got some toys and things," he added. "And umm...if you could take the dress off and just wear your underwear, that would be great."

I followed his guidance, walking into the bathroom and noticing the small suitcase that lay on the counter.

"When you're ready," he finally said, smiling warmly. "I'm yours to do with as you see fit." With that, he tugged the door closed and left me in the brightly lit room.

I stared at the case for a while, worried about opening it. I was sure to find items there that were completely foreign to me. My knowledge of BDSM toys was very limited. Prolonging the inevitable, I decided to reach around my back and unzip my dress instead. Shrugging my shoulders out of the material, I allowed it to fall to the ground and carefully stepped out of it. My underwear were exactly what he'd asked for: a scarlet lace bra, which barely concealed my nipples, and matching boy short panties.

I swiveled, checking myself in the large mirror above the sink. And then, there was nothing else to do. The moment I'd be dreading could be put off no longer. Grabbing the zipper of the suitcase, I ripped it around quickly as though I was tearing off a band-aid. Then, tossing the cover off, I stared at the contents. Some of it wasn't as frightening as I'd imagined, a paddle, a whip, some handcuffs, a blindfold and a ball gag. However, there were also toys I'd only ever seen pictures of online: a butt plug, a cock ring, a dildo. Would he want me to use all of this stuff?

Swallowing, my brain buzzed quickly. I tried to come up with a few things to say to him; tasks I'd get him to do in order to humiliate him before I even considered pulling out some of the more fancy tricks.

I reminded myself that it was just a matter of sliding into a role, pretending that I was someone else. If I could get into the mindset of a dominant woman, everything else would fall into place. So, with that, I breathed deeply, altered my posture so that I stood more erect. I watched in the mirror, as my face took on a hardened, no-nonsense expression. Nodding curtly, at my reflection, I reached for the door and flung it open. It moved so quickly that the knob bashed hard against the bathroom counter. I remember thinking that was good. I certainly made an entrance.

Steven was sitting on the edge of the bed, but shot to his feet when he heard the bang of the door. His eyes widened as they focused on me.

I stood with my feet shoulder-width apart, balancing on my heels, and placed one hand on my hip. "What are you doing still dressed?" I asked as sharply as I could muster, arching one eyebrow as my gaze moved down the length of his body.

"I...I..." he blabbered, his entire demeanor changed. Just moments before, he'd seemed reasonably confident; certainly more in control of the situation that I'd been. But he could no longer find his words and, it seemed, the prospect of being humiliated had already brought out the submissive side of him. He looked almost scared of me.

I didn't understand how such a change could happen so quickly in him, but it gave me the boost in confidence I needed. As I watched his body and saw the slight swell at his groin, it spurred me onto greater assertiveness. "I said, why are you dressed?" I repeated.

"I'm sorry Mistress Arianna," he rapidly mumbled, his fingers moving to the hem of his golf shirt and tugging it from his jeans.

"Did I say you could take them off?" I don't know where that came from. The truth is, I don't know where anything I said or did that night came from. I lost myself to the part I was playing. Suddenly, as if a switch had been flicked, I no longer needed to think about what I was saying before I said it.

"Umm," he muttered, his fingers slowly releasing the fabric.

"Did I say you could speak?" I demanded.

He moved his head from side to side a little shakily.

"You don't talk unless I give you permission to," I told him, my hand falling from my hip as I took a step toward him. "You're my little bitch, understand?" I didn't raise my voice, it didn't seem necessary. I had his complete attention, and the words seemed to have more effect when spoken calmly, but firmly.

He nodded eagerly, his eyes latching onto the curve of my breasts.

"You may speak," I smoothly said.

"Yes, yes," he replied, stumbling as he quickly tripped over the word. "I understand, Mistress. I am your bitch."

"That's good," I quietly responded, rewarding him with a small smile. "Now," I added. "I want you to get those clothes off." Folding my arms beneath my bosom, I stood within arm's reach of him.

He lapped quickly at his bottom lip, before eagerly grabbing the bottom of his shirt. He tugged it quickly over his head, revealing a toned torso with wisps of dark gray hair. He unbuttoned his jeans, pulled down the zipper and pushed them off his hips. His briefs, which were black, were growing tighter around his groin, as he continued to gradually grow harder. His eyes flicked at me, as he kicked the denim from his feet and his hands grabbed the waistband of his underpants.

"Take them off," I ordered, sensing that he wanted another push.

I saw the flash of something in his eye that told me he was turned on by the instruction. And obediently, he shoved the briefs off his hips. They too ended up at his ankles and he kicked them off too. He now stood before me, naked except for a pair of black socks that came to his mid-calf.

My gaze moved upward, focusing on the semi-erect penis that was continuing to stir. His intact foreskin hadn't retracted completely, but the soft pink of his gland was beginning to emerge. He had a very thick vein running along the top of his shaft and a patch of bushy graying hair just above it. His scrotum was quite large, the skin dark and slightly wrinkled.

Taking a small step, I reached out and cupped his testicles in the palm of my right hand. I stared into his eyes as I squeezed gently.

His own gaze went a little glassy, and he tried to hold back a quiet groan.

"You like that?" I asked, with a knowing grin playing at my lips.

Another muted grunt and a nod was all he gave in response.

"You want it harder?"

"Ugh," he mumbled, sucking in a breath as I rolled his balls between my fingers. Then, in jerky movements, he nodded in reply to my question.

Remembering one of the most important facets of BDSM and humiliation, I quickly withdrew my hand. "Beg for it," I told him bluntly.

He was breathing quickly and raggedly through his nose. His penis was becoming completely hard, rising in a curve that pointed almost directly at the ceiling. "Please," he weakly mumbled.

"You can do better than that," I urged, stepping back.

"Please, Mistress," he breathlessly began. "Please."

"You call that begging?" I scoffed. "Get on your knees and do it properly."

Instantly, Steven lowered himself to the hotel's cream carpet, his pupils dancing as his arousal heightened. Dropping onto all fours, he shuffled forward slightly. "Please," he said earnestly. "Touch me," he pleaded. "Squeeze me hard," he haltingly added. "Hurt me."

I ordered him to get back up and as soon as he was standing, I complied with his request. Grasping his tender flesh, I dug my fingers in, using the slightest pressure of my fingernails.

"Oh, God," he panted excitedly, his eyes closing and his head dropping back until his face was directed to the ceiling.

Emboldened, I gripped a little tighter. "Who said you could talk?" I said darkly, slowly twisting my hand.

"Ugh, ugh, ugh," he grunted with an exhale of breath on each sound.

After a few seconds more, I released him, leaving red marks were my hand had been and tiny pricks of broken skin where two of my nails had punctured him.

Causing him pain, in of itself, didn't excite me. However, the fact that causing him pain had resulted in his intense arousal and pleasure most definitely did. He was panting heavily, as if the experience had been orgasmic. With the courage to try more, I told him to wait, while I returned to the bathroom.

When I got back to him, I had several things in my hands; a pair of handcuffs, a paddle and the dildo. I wasn't exactly sure what I was planning to do with the latter. But, I figured, if it was in his bag of toys, it must be something he enjoys using.

"Do you remember," I began slowly, "when I told you not to speak unless I gave you permission?"

He nodded, swallowing nervously.

"Well, you disobeyed me," I added, with a regretful smile. "So, now you're going to have to be punished."

"I-" he mumbled, shaking his head.

"I didn't say you could speak," I sharply reminded him. "Obviously, you need to be taught to listen to my instructions." Tossing the dildo and the paddle onto the bed, I kept the handcuffs tightly held in my left hand. "Go over to the wall," I said, pointing with my empty hand to the head of the bed.

His eyes watching me over his shoulder, he did as directed, walking until his feet bumped the bedside cabinet.

"Right there," I assured him. "Now lift your arms," I demanded.

His restless tongue darted out to moisten his lips again, before his hands slowly rose toward his head. I grabbed his left hand, the one closest to me, and snapped one cuff around it. Clamping the metal bracelet shut, I pushed his hand to the wall and the light fitting that was positioned three feet or so above the cabinet.

The light was a sleek modern design, with bulbs on either end of a thick rod of steel, or something that looked like steel. That center rod was attached to the wall at either end, with a small gap in the middle. I looped the cuff through this gap and ordered Steven to lift his other wrist into the open bracelet.

He did so without hesitation or argument and I quickly closed the cuffs; yanking on them to ensure they were secure. With his upper arms now masking half his face, he continued to peer expectantly over his shoulder at me. I moved back to the foot of the bed, completely out of his view, before picking up the paddle.

I considered waiting, knowing that the longer it was dragged out, the more the anticipation would be killing him. I could already see the glistening streaks of sweat weaving their way down his smooth back.

His buttocks were rounder and fuller than the average man's, and as he unconsciously clenched them a small dimple appeared in each. No longer able to hold back, I walked forward to him. Flicking the paddle and brought it down hard on his right cheek. At least, I thought it was hard, the sound that filled the room was feeble and unsatisfying – my guess would be for both of us.

So, I pulled back and tried again, giving myself a larger windup. This time, it struck his skin with a 'thwap' and caused him to jerk slightly. It was followed by a rumble low in his chest. I struck him again and again, each time pausing for no more than a few seconds. All the time, I listened closely to his breathing, and watched the movement of his body. His desperate, loud exhalations were highly sexual. And despite my early concerns, I was not only slipping into the role, I was enjoying it. There was something incredibly arousing about control.

"Argh," he cried, his hands balling into tight fists and his biceps flexing.

"Do you want to say something?" I suggested, my own breath coming fast and uneven from a mixture of titillation and exertion. My upper arm was burning from the unfamiliar exercise, and as I tossed the paddle back onto the bed, I was glad to be able to stretch the fingers that had been clamped tightly around the handle.

"Ugh, Mistress," he grunted. "I need..." he gasped. "Please touch me."

"Not yet," I stated calmly. It would surely be an anticlimax for him if I gave into his request in the first instance. "I think there's still some punishment that needs to be doled out." Unaware that I was doing it, I was reaching down to the bed and scooping up the six inch, pink dildo that he'd packed in the case. "You need to know who's boss," I added, wrapping my fingers tightly around the handle and moving closer to him.

He whimpered as I rolled the head of the phallus over his buttock, warning him of what was about to happen. His hips were involuntarily swaying, backwards and forwards in a light thrusting motion that suggested to me he was ready.

Carefully, I slide the dildo down and placed it against his pucker. "You're a dirty, little bitch," I whispered, my face almost resting on his shoulder.

"Mmm," he hummed, keeping his jaw clamped shut.

"You may speak," I told him.

"Yes," he exhaled. "Yes, I am dirty."

"You want this?" I asked, pushing the head of the plastic penis against his tight hole.

"Argh, God, Yes!" he almost screamed.

My movements were slow, not shoving against the resistance I found, but letting his body slowly draw the dildo in. With my free hand, I reached around him, stroking the underside of his cock with the tips of my fingers. He bucked against me, grunting as he bit down on his lip. As I reached the soft, smooth dome of his tip, he quivered and the dildo slipped a couple of inches deeper.

"Who's your mistress?" I asked, releasing his member.

"Ugh, you," he panted, sweat running from him freely. "You," he repeated.

I flood of warmth and moisture pooled in the crotch of my underwear, making me feel restless, as I instantly placed my legs together and squeezed my thighs. It wasn't the words he said, but the strangled way in which he'd spoken them that was almost enough to make me orgasm right then and there. The power I held over him was intoxicating.

With one more push, I slipped the dildo into Steven's depths. What I hadn't known at the time was my over excitement would prove too much for him.

With a growled, "Argh...ugh...ugh!" Steven's member lengthened and released its seed. His ejaculate coating the surface of the bedside cabinet and splattering the wall.

And that, as they say, was that.

Chapter Four
Big Guy

After Steven's sudden climax, he could not muster another erection. He wanted to; he tried; we both tired, but he was spent. And although he would have liked to have spent a little more time playing, he seemed very satisfied with the date. Before I left him, with the ink on a check still drying, he also gave me his card; with a work and cell phone number.

"Please call me whenever you're free," he smiled. "I...umm...don't think I'll need to be finding any one else until you retire," he added, with a wink.

"Thanks," I replied, gratefully taking the card and slipping it and the check into my purse. However, unlike, Steven I didn't leave entirely satisfied. I was glad that I'd managed to perform well for him, way beyond my expectations, but I was desperate for a release of my own. So much so that when I got to the underground parking lot, I slipped into the back seat of my car so I could stretch out and masturbate myself to a brief orgasm that was just enough to see me through the journey home. Unlike my date with David, at no time did I feel the sense of satisfaction and completeness. Instead, I found myself craving the sensation of being filled.

Over the next couple of days, I played with myself on five more occasions, each time thinking about my experience with Steven. It was not until the day of my next date, with John, that I began to allow my mind to drift from the memory.

My appointment with John took place at a not quite so ritzy hotel. Not that the standard of the place mattered; it was, importantly, out of the way, quiet and clean. It was a privately owned establishment and he requested that I meet him in the parking lot, so we could sign in together.

He quickly approached me, greeting me with a nervous smile. He was a heavily-built man in his early forties. He wasn't particularly fat, but he had a very thick frame, with ridiculously wide shoulders. He was tall, too. Easily six and a half feet, maybe even bigger than that. His hair was receding and what little he had was shaved close to his scalp. All told, he looked like the kind of man who would be a bouncer or bodyguard.

At the reception desk, he introduced us as husband and wife to the elderly lady who was the receptionist and owner. He then handed over a credit card and signed in. I never asked him why he felt the need to have the veneer of 'proper' to us sharing a room. I don't suppose it mattered; it was just another peculiarity of people.

John was different from the other men I'd met; he didn't want to talk; didn't want to eat or have a drink. It seemed to me that perhaps he was not as affluent as my other two clients had been, he appeared to be very aware of the fact that I was already on the clock and he wanted to get down to the main event.

At another time, that may have bothered me, but with the longing in my loins that had been burning for three days, the lack of finesse with which he began to paw at my clothes didn't trouble me at all.

This time, I'd chosen to go without any underwear, and as his hand pushed my skirt off my hips and met naked skin he seemed to approve.

"I like a girl who comes prepared," he remarked, his eyes moving down to my waxed mound. His right hand swept rapidly between my legs, the heel of his hand pushing possessively at my sex.

"I aim to please," I told him, holding eye contact with him, as he worked his coarse fingers between my lips and sought my entrance.

"Hmm," he hummed, sliding a second chubby finger inside. "It's nice," he mumbled. "Nice and tight."

I shuffled my left leg, spreading wider for him. "It's all yours," I tempted him.

"Fuck," he whispered. "I want to bang you so hard."

"You can do whatever you want with me," I responded, smiling. "I'm yours."

As arousal caused his chest to start heaving, he pulled his hand away from my body. Hurriedly, he started to remove his clothing, shrugging out of a charcoal jacket and then moving to the buttons on his shirt. I didn't help him. Instead, I continued to keep my eyes on his, giving him a sultry smile, as I kicked off my shoes and stepped out of the puddle of skirt at my feet.

It took him no longer than ten seconds to strip completely. Somehow he looked even larger without clothes, with huge bulging biceps that wouldn't allow his arms to sit by his sides. His shaft, however, was an average size. Or maybe it was slightly larger and just looked average on him. I couldn't be sure without a tape measure, and it didn't seem right to ask him if we could stop so I could measure it.

"Oh, fuck, baby," he muttered, stepping forward and grabbing my hips with both of his large strong hands. "I want you so bad."

"Uh uh," I reminded him carefully, pointing down at his member. "One more thing before we can get this party started," I said.

"Shit," he cursed, his hands refusing to let go and his face drifting closer to mine., "I forgot," he whispered his lips almost brushing mine. "Can't we do it just this once without, huh? I swear I'm clean."

I didn't believe him – not about being clean, he might have been telling the truth about that. But I didn't believe he'd forgotten to bring a condom. I think he was just one of the many men who don't like wearing them and hoped that perhaps he could talk his way around it.

"I never do that," I told him calmly with a small smile. "It's for the safety of my clients as well as my own," I pointed out. "But, lucky for you, I always carry a few." Placing my hands over his, I deliberately removed his grasp of me. I moved over to a small table with a wobbly leg and opened my purse. Quickly I put my hands on a condom wrapper and ripped it open. I returned to him, holing the circle of latex between my finger and thumb. I grinned at him, as I fell to my knees. "I promise it'll still feel good," I added, noting the disappointed look on his face.

The Escort Next Door

I leaned forward and teasingly ran my tongue in a circle over his head, before slipping the condom over him. Then, I squeezed his shaft gently as I smoothed it down to his base.

He jerked and shivered as I did so, muttering a string of curses under his breath.

"There now," I softly said, pushing myself to my feet. "We're ready to rock and roll."

With a snap of motion, his hands were back on my hips and he was turning me around. Then, with one stride he pushed me to the floral wallpapered wall. It was the kind with an embossed pattern, which was pressing uncomfortably into the skin of my back. However, there was no time to complain about it. He was already using his tremendous strength to lift me. My back slipped at least a foot up the wall, and I instinctively wrapped my ankles around the small of his back.

"Ohh," I squealed in surprise.

"You smell good," he mumbled, placing his nose to my shoulder and inhaling deeply. "Damn it, I want to fuck your brains out." As he said that, he took one hand off me.

Sure I was about to fall, I grabbed his sturdy shoulders with both hands. However, it seemed he could just as easily take my weight with only one arm, while he grabbed the shaft of his erection and positioned it at my glistening, moist channel.

He started slowly, pushing himself in a little at a time, which drove me crazy with anticipation. When he completed his entrance with a grunt of pleasure, I felt myself open completely to him, I wailed for what he'd promised.

"Fuck me," I begged. "Fuck me!"

"Yeah, baby," he grunted, giving an extra push to ensure he was as deep as he could get. Then, there was a flurry of action.

His hips moved like a piston, pumping relentless; his body slapping hard against mine, my back banging against the wall with a thud on each completed thrust. He wasn't lazy; making sure to pull almost completely from me before ramming back to the hilt.

My mouth hung perpetually open, releasing a moan each time the air was pushed from my lungs. He growled aggressively with each drive of his hips, and the masculine scent of his sweat and arousal drifted up from our joined bodies.

"Oh, yeah," I began to mewl. "Give it to me!" With each slide of his cock within me, I felt energized. And each bump of his pubic bone against my clitoris sent me spiraling higher. I was on the verge of orgasm, bucking against him with almost as much force as he was thrusting into me. "Yes," I panted. "Oh, Christ, yes! Yes!"

Spots began to dance in front of my closed eyelids. It was a strange kind of rolling orgasm; it didn't come in one big bang, but just kept drifting back and forth with every explosive ram of his pubic bone against mine. The seconds went by and I remained in that state of bliss, still crying out and moaning. It began to feel as though it could last forever.

Only it didn't last forever. John stopped moving inside me. Carefully he scooped me up and stepped back towards the bed. There, he promptly dropped me and his cock slipped out of me.

"You are one sexy woman," he muttered, placing his hands on my waist and flipping me over onto my stomach. Once I was there, he coaxed me onto my hands and knees.

I glanced over my shoulder, watching him with orgasm fogged eyes as he placed himself between my legs.

"You like it like this?" he asked, a mischievous grin spreading across his face, as he poked his still rock hard member to my asshole.

Quickly reaching around I grabbed his dick before he had a chance to do anything else. Heart pounding in my chest, I tried not to appear as frightened by the prospect as I was. "It's going to cost you extra," I said, hoping that would be enough to put him off the idea. I'd never engaged in any kind of anal play and despite the way Steven had apparently enjoyed it, I wasn't sure I was quite ready for that step. At least not with the lumberjack approach John was taking.

"How much?" he asked thoughtfully.

"Another thousand," I said calmly. It didn't feel odd that we were discussing a business transaction, while naked, with me on all fours and him kneeling at my butt.

Solemnly, he shook his head. "All right, I'll stick with your pussy."

"Your choice," I shrugged, releasing my grip of him, and trying to give the impression that I had a blasé attitude towards anal sex. That way, he would know that it was his decision not to go through with it, and that I, being an excellent escort, had given him everything he'd wanted.

"We'll do that another time maybe," he shrugged. It was clear that he was disappointed and I wondered if his enthusiasm had started to wane.

With a jolt of my hips, I bumped my backside against him. "Come on, big boy," I throatily said. "Finish what you started."

"You still want more, you little slut?" he asked.

"I can take all you've got to offer," I promised, giving him one more bump with my buttocks.

The Escort Next Door

This spurred him into sudden action once more. He angrily gripped my waist and pushed himself into my waiting sex. "Ugh," he howled. "God, your pussy is so warm," he grunted. "So soft."

I was even wetter from my prolonged orgasm, and as he quickly pumped, our combined groans and moans were accompanied by the soft squelch of his body disappearing within mine. At any other time in my life, I would have found that sound effect embarrassing, but it seemed perfectly natural given the rough, animalistic sex we were having. In fact, it even turned me on.

"Harder," I said, encouraging him to give me everything he'd got.

Pinching my waist more tightly, he shouted, as he stepped up the speed and depth of his thrusts. In this new position, the angle of his tip rubbed manically against my G-spot. It brought with it a much more violent orgasm that knocked the strength from me. My upper half flopped forward, collapsing on the bed. The only thing keeping my lower half up was his strong hands. With the stamina of a stallion, he continued to thrust as I rode the sensation. However, the strength of my internal spams soon milked him.

With a cry of, "Fuck, fuck, fuck," and then a muttered, "So good!" he rammed his cock into my channel three more times, before the spasms of his body gripped him. With strangled breaths, he pulled from me and fell back onto the bed.

Without his support, I flopped onto my stomach, my own breath ragged. "God," I mumbled, turning my face away from the pillow. "Wow," I added with a chuckle. "That was incredible."

"You're incredible," he replied, his voice sounding very far away. Yet I knew he couldn't be, because the weight of one of his legs was still on mine.

It wasn't until I was slipping out half an hour and a shower later that I realized the little old lady may have thought we were married, but the noises coming from the room were enough to shock the God-fearing life out of her anyway.

CHAPTER FIVE

STUDENT

On Paul's return, I remembered to behave exactly as I had before I found out about his affairs. I wrapped my arms around him when he walked through the door, I tried to talk to him about the trip, that night I attempted to instigate sex. It all worked like a charm, he treated me with cold indifference and shrugged off my attempts at intimacy. I breathed a sigh of relief, realizing if the plan had backfired, I would have found myself in a situation I really didn't want to be in.

It may seem strange to say, but I was happy to sleep with strangers who could have had sex with numerous women – even on the very day that I met them. But it wasn't so much about the physical act, although with Paul it would have been unprotected, so that did change things somewhat. No, my main concern was the fact that Paul had betrayed me.

Selling my body was fine when both parties knew that that was the score. Giving myself unwillingly to a man who'd lied; the man who claimed to love me. No, that was very different in my mind.

To my disappointment, Paul's trips seemed to have temporarily dried up. My guess is this was a huge blow to him, too. And it wasn't just the fun I'd be missing out on. I had a bigger problem. Through word of mouth, my reputation was growing. I had another three potential new clients, all of whom were keen to see me within the next few days. What's more, hearing from their friends the rate I charged, they were offering to pay more to encourage me to break any existing dates I'd scheduled.

I was now being offered three thousand dollars (and more) per hour. It was simply too good to pass up. However, there was a problem. How could I spend the night out without Paul wondering where I was? I had to think very carefully about that.

It didn't take long though for a plan to formulate in my mind. Paul was working in his den when I approached him on a Wednesday afternoon. He'd decided not to go into the office and had been working from home the last few days.

The Escort Next Door

"Hey, honey," I began, walking in with a cup of steaming coffee in my hand. "I thought you might like a little refreshment," I suggested.

"Thanks," he muttered, not looking up from his laptop, his fingers still scurrying over the keys.

Placing the mug on his desk, I lingered for a moment, hoping he would acknowledge my presence. He didn't. "Umm," I began. "I was wondering if you'd mind staying here with the kids tomorrow night, so I can go to the gym?"

"The gym?" he replied, still only half paying attention.

"Yeah," I responded. "It's been a long time since I've had the chance and I'm starting to feel a little flabby," I mentioned, looking down at my abdomen to add conviction to the story.

"I think you are, too," he replied, without any trace of humor. He finally lifted his eyes from the computer screen and met my face for a moment. "I think it's a good idea," he nodded. "You could do with getting a few hours exercise."

I quashed the urge to ask him what he meant by that, to argue that I looked hot for having had three children and that there were plenty of men who thought so. All of that stayed in my head. What came out of my mouth was a simple, "Thanks." I tried not to add a dash of sarcasm to it and I attempted a genuine smile. "I won't leave until after dinner and bedtime," I explained. "So might not be back till midnight or later."

"Fine, whatever," he said dismissively, returning his focus to his work.

Although it hurt to think he cared so little about what I was doing, it was incredibly helpful to my plan. So, I didn't spend too long licking the wound.

The following evening, I met Chris. He was a twenty-three-year-old student, with very wealthy parents by all accounts. I thought he was probably a trust-fund baby. He told me in his email that he lacked any confidence with women, and it had been a while since he'd last had sex.

Neither of these things were problematic to me. They might have been earlier on, but I was beginning to gain real confidence in my body, my sexuality and my ability to give pleasure to men no matter what their tastes.

Strangely, Chris asked me to come to his apartment, rather than meeting in neutral territory. I explained that I don't make a habit of doing that, for safety reasons. However, something about his messages seemed genuine and I felt that I could trust him.

His home, at least I assumed it was *his* home (perhaps he had enough money to rent a condo for a night), was a massive luxurious bachelor pad, right in the middle of the busy city. It was only an hour's drive from my house, which was a little closer than I'd become comfortable with working, but it meant that, with a bit of luck, I'd be able to get back before the early hours of the morning.

Chris was a big guy, quite substantially overweight. As he answered the door, he was a little breathless from the walk. He was very fresh-faced, looking quite a bit younger than he claimed, but given what he would go on to tell me, I have no reason to believe he'd lie about his age. His hair was a light brown, styled in a mock 1950s pompadour. He wore nicely tailored clothes, despite his size. And I couldn't help but notice the platinum Rolex on his left wrist.

"Arianna?" he asked.

"That's me," I smiled. "It's a pleasure to meet you Chris," I added, offering him my right hand.

He took it in his sweaty palm and anxiously shook it. "Pleasure to meet you," he echoed. "Please, come on in."

I wandered into a large high-ceilinged living space, with white leather couches surrounding an open fire place. "This is very nice," I noted.

"Thanks," he replied. "Please take a seat."

After giving him a grateful nod, I sashayed to one of the couches and sat on the edge, keeping one hand on the hem of my dress as I lowered myself. I got the distinct impression he was watching me closely as I moved, his eyes seemed to burn into me. Rather than make me feel self-conscious, it made me feel good – really good.

"Like I said in my email," he began, taking a seat on the couch opposite me. "I don't really know what to do with women. They're not exactly falling at my feet," he self-deprecatingly muttered, gesturing to his body. "It's hard for me to meet someone." He was quiet for a few seconds, but I sensed there was something else he wanted to say, so I deliberately didn't fill the silence. "And, umm, I have needs...Well, I suppose I don't need to tell you that," he said, shaking his head at what he felt was his own stupidity.

"We all have needs Chris," I reminded him. "And as for being attractive to women," I added, smiling warmly. "You'll find that looks aren't the most important thing to a lot of them."

"Well," he mumbled hesitantly. "My experience suggests differently." Again, a small spell of silence descended on that large room. It was quiet enough to hear a pin drop. He shuffled in his seat, drawing a hand through his thick, gelled hair. "You see, I've only ever..." he lost steam as things began to get tricky. "I've only ever...Once," he mumbled, his eyes focused on my feet.

"You're still young," I reminded him. "There's plenty of time,"

"Maybe" he said, clearly unconvinced. "But this one time, it was just pity sex. A friend I went to high school with agreed to pop my cherry, but it was...well, it wasn't anything like I imagined."

"First times rarely are," I assured him, sympathetically.

"Anyway," he sighed. "That was nearly three years ago, and since then...Nothing."

"Okay," I said calmly, ensuring that he knew none of these things were a problem. "So what is it that you want from me? Anything special, I mean. Do you have particular tastes, fantasies?"

He looked panicked, his eyes moving quickly to my face. "I...I just want to have sex," he muttered weakly, seeming worried that his answer wouldn't please me.

"That's fine," I nodded. "If there's anything that you think of, just let me know. Okay?" I was getting to my feet, and as I did so, he looked a bit like a deer caught in the headlights.

"You wanna?" he blurted. "I mean, now?"

"We can do whatever you want to do, Chris," I quickly tried to sooth his concern. "If you want to sit and talk some more, we can do that. But I think it's one of those things that won't get any easier no matter how long you wait."

"Oh," he whispered.

"You just need to relax, Chris. There's no pressure and I promise everything will be fine."

"O...Okay," he stumbled.

I moved to him, placing my hand on his shoulder when I was within reach. Slowly, I moved my hand up to his neck and then caressed the underneath of his chin. This caused him to lift his face to mine. Making no sudden movements, I bent my head to his and gently pressed my lips to his.

He made no effort to kiss me back, still too scared to do anything but sit there like a stunned possum. His eyes however, showed the agitation and arousal that was brewing beneath them. His gaze drifted to my cleavage which was eye-level as I bent over him.

"You like what you see?" I asked, reaching down and slipping my fingers over the back of his right hand.

"I didn't," he quickly uttered, shaking his head. "I mean I was, but I didn't mean to."

"It's fine," I chuckled good-naturedly, lifting his hand leisurely to my face. I turned it over, dropping a kiss into the palm, before moving it back down to my chest. As I pressed his fingers to my left breast, he shuddered and sucked in a quaking breath. "You like that?" I asked rhetorically.

He didn't respond verbally, but his eyes fixed on the flesh beneath his fingers and he nodded.

I guided his hand, showing him how to cup the breast, and encouraging him to massage it. "Don't be frightened," I told him. "It won't bite."

With a much need release of nerves, Chris laughed lightly at the joke. "I just, I don't know how hard," he said, voicing his concern.

"No two women are exactly alike, we all enjoy being touched in different ways," I told him, still calmly guiding his hand over the globe of flesh beneath it. "But it's best to treat them with care," I added. "Firm, but gentle."

"Firm, but gentle," he echoed, committing the statement to memory, as he clenched his fingers lightly and squeezed me.

"Hmmm," I moaned. "That's the right kind of thing."

He gasped at the noise of pleasure, and his breath became more labored. Glancing down, I saw that there was already a large tent in his pants. When he noticed my line of sight, he quickly tried to cover his groin with his free hand.

"There's nothing to be ashamed of," I assured him. "After all, that's an important part of the process."

"It's just too soon," he muttered. "I shouldn't be this excited so soon, should I?"

"Chris," I sighed, releasing my hold of his hand and sinking to my knees. "There are no rules to this. Everyone is different, some men take a little longer to get ready than others. Young men, like you, can usually get aroused pretty quickly. And I think just about every man who ever walked the face of the planet has had it suddenly happen when they don't want it to."

"So," he said weakly. "You're not upset?"

"Of course, I'm not," I told him, reaching out to remove the hand that was trying unsuccessfully to mask his erection. "Why don't you let me help you with that?" I suggested, taking his hand to his knee and depositing it there.

His pants were straining at his waist, because of his husky size. It didn't bother me. I simply aimed for his zipper and pulled it gently down. "Just relax," I reminded him, looking up into his concerned face once more. "Trust me."

With his fly open, I carefully reached between the folds of fabric and found the opening of his boxers. Without the aid of my eyes, I found the tiny button and popped that open, too. It was then easy, to place my fingers around his shaft and guide it through the gaps in his clothes. I felt him tremble as I touched him, and his cock jolted even more violently when it was brought out into the open air.

It, like the rest of him, was stout, but I would guess that if he lost weight, his dick would remain the same. It had a really nice girth to it, the kind of size that could really give a woman pleasure. "Hmm," I hummed my approval. "This is nice," I told him.

"Really?" he asked, quickly. "You're not just saying that, because I'm paying you?" he added gracelessly.

"No," I insisted. "It's a nice size, not too big but plenty big enough" I told him. "Smooth and soft," I added, as my hand wrapped around him and stroked from the base to the head. "Straight," I whispered, smoothing my hands back down on the return journey.

Chris was panting, his hands gripping the fabric of his pants. "Ugh, please," he mumbled. "I don't think I-"

I knew what was happening; knew he wanted me to stop before it did. But I thought it would be better in the long run to get it out of the way.

"Arhh," he groaned, as his penis lengthened and four strong spurts of semen shot from the head in long ropes that splashed my face, the section of chest exposed in my dress and the dress itself. "Oh, shit," he mumbled. "I'm so sorry, I didn't mean to-"

"Shhh," I hushed him, sitting up so I could kiss him on the mouth. "I told you to relax," I smiled. "It's perfectly natural, you said it had been a long time. There was a lot of pressure needing to be released," I chuckled, looking deliberately down at my splattered body and clothes. "Now, when we go again, you'll be able to last longer," I informed him.

"Again?" he asked, breathlessly.

"Yeah," I nodded. "We're not done yet," I promised him. "This is just the beginning."

Chapter Six

Teacher

Over the following three weeks, I saw Chris on five more occasions. Paul was perfectly satisfied that I'd spent those evenings at the gym. And although I always took a sports bag with me, I was grateful it didn't ever seem to strike him as strange that I didn't leave the house dressed for a work out. In fact, I don't suppose he noticed what I'd been wearing at all.

But much more importantly than what was or wasn't registering with Paul, Chris was growing in confidence with each date. As he began to relax, he was able to keep his ejaculation at bay for longer stretches at a time. I choose to move gradually though, first treating him to leisurely periods of fellatio before moving on to penetration. I had a hunch that the sensation of vaginal sex would be intense and he'd once again experience premature ejaculation.

I'd told him to relax and let me do the work. But, sure enough, the first time I lowered myself onto his chunky erection, he almost immediately shuddered, jerked and filled the condom he'd been wearing. However, thanks to the fifteen minutes he'd managed to last when I'd performed orally for him four days before, I was able to convince him that it was no big deal.

"You can last longer," I told him. "You just need to get used to that pressure."

He was panting, his fingers trembling violently, as he tried to hold onto my hips. "I...I...Oh, God," he mumbled. "It's so tight," he gasped. "It was just too much, I couldn't hold it back," he added between deep, ragged breaths.

"It's okay," I soothed, gently stroking my fingers at the back of his head. "Next time it'll be better."

That had become my mantra, and clichéd though it may have seemed to him, he knew that it was true, because he'd seen the evidence of it. Over the course of our next two dates, we had sex four times; each one lasting a little longer than the first. During our final encounter, I began to encourage him to take control. He was worried that his size would hinder him, but I tenderly proved him wrong by showing him several positions that worked well. He seemed to particularly enjoy a sideways entry with me lying on my side, with my knees drawn up close to my chest. He was able to kneel on the mattress by my butt. After slipping a pillow under my hips, we were good to go. While able to control the speed and depth of his own thrusts, I told him to slow down or even stop if he felt the desire to ejaculate becoming too strong.

He was a wonderful student, eager to learn and, by the time he'd got to grips with controlling the response of his own body, he wanted to know how to give pleasure to a woman. I gently explained that all women are different, as are their tastes, but I gave him a brief introduction to the clitoris and the G-spot.

When we were next due to meet, he surprised me by handing over a much larger stack of bills than usual. "Umm," I smiled, peering down at the cash, which was a thousand dollars more than I charged him for an evening. "What's all this?" I asked, chuckling.

"It's a parting gift," he said, smiling a little bashfully.

"Parting?"

"Yeah," he nodded. "See, I...umm...well, I've met someone and I just think it wouldn't be right to keep meeting with you."

I grinned warmly. I didn't have to pretend to be pleased for him; I really was. Chris was obviously the kind of man who was desperate for the security and support of a relationship. Sure, he enjoyed sex, but to him, I think, it felt mechanical when there was no real love attached to it. He'd found himself caught between a rock and a hard place, feeling inadequate sexually had made him reluctant to get involved with anyone. He needed a guiding hand from a woman he wasn't in love with; a woman who he didn't *have* to please in order to keep. It had all worked out very well.

"I mean," he added, "it's not that I don't want to see you anymore. For a while there...." he scoffed at himself, before leaving the sentence unfinished. "Anyway," he briskly sighed. "I don't wanna risk messing things up with this girl and it would just feel wrong, you know?"

Nodding, I dropped the cash onto the thick glass coffee table and stepped forward. "I'm so pleased for you," I told him, smoothly wrapping both arms around his waist and pulling him toward me.

He returned the hug, but seemed uncomfortable. It was only a second before he was pulling back.

As he did, I realized what the problem was – a huge erection. "Well," I chuckled. "I think someone else wants to say goodbye." I reached for his belt, but he quickly stepped back.

"I can't," he said. "It really has to end now. I don't want cheat on this girl."

"But," I smiled, jerking my thumb over my shoulder toward my purse. "You've paid me for tonight. And some!"

"Yeah," he nodded, smiling. "I wanted to thank you, for everything." Drawing his fingers through his always perfectly style hair, he shuffled awkwardly on the spot. "I know I owe you so much more than that, but I hope it goes someway to repaying you."

I didn't see Chris again after that. I never found out how things turned out with his girlfriend. I hope they're still together and he's found happiness. He was a sweet soul; nothing like I'd expected when I realized he was a rich, young man who had never, and would never, have to work a day in his life. Some men stay with me, I still think about them often and I wish I could have met them under different circumstances – Chris is one of those men.

Weeks quickly turned into months and as the late summer heat gave way to a decidedly chilly fall, I was probably happier than I'd ever been in my life. Paul hadn't been away for several weeks, but he still spent a lot of time at the office and very little at home. There were a couple of occasions when the lack of opportunity for his clandestine affairs caused him to try to instigate sex with me. The first time, I'd told him I had a mild bladder infection. A complete lie, but it was certainly enough to put him off the idea of making love. The second time, almost a month later, Paul had stood behind me while I was brushing my hair. Gradually, he rubbed his fingers over my shoulders, before working his way around to my breasts. It was Dylan who saved the day by barging into our bedroom without knocking, as had become his habit.

"Damn it," Paul yelled, his hands snapping away from me and his whole body moving angrily to the doorway. "How many times?" he bellowed.

Poor Dylan looked wide-eyed between his furious father and me. This time, quite the opposite from being upset with him, I was grateful.

"What's the matter sweetie?" I asked, slowly getting up from the stool at my dressing table and calmly approaching.

Paul's anger was not abating. "I'm serious, Dylan. How many times?"

Gripping Paul's arm, I coaxed him away from our startled son. "Let me handle this," I urged.

"Because you've handled it so fucking well in the past?" he shouted, quite loudly enough for the neighbors to hear, never mind our four-year-old, who was standing not three feet away.

I was about to say something about his choice of language, but with a huff of resignation, I simply turned away from him and offered my open right hand to my little boy.

Dylan took it obediently, and let himself be led from the bedroom. "Why is Daddy so mad at me?" he whispered as we walked a little way down the hall.

"Oh, it's not just you, sweetheart," I shook my head. "He's mad at me, too. He's just in a bad mood, that's all."

"I'm sorry that I didn't knock," he dolefully added. "I thought I saw something in my room and...and I was scared, so I just-"

"It's okay," I quickly offered. "I know you didn't mean any harm. Dad knows that, too. He just needs some time to calm down."

I thoroughly checked Dylan's room for any signs of monsters and ghosts. There was nothing, and I attempted to explain what he thought he saw by gesturing to the shadows that came from moonlight filtering through the bottom of his curtains. Eventually, he seemed to believe me, and climbed back into bed.

When I returned to our bedroom, the door was slightly ajar. I thought I heard a breathless pant, so didn't waltz right in. Instead, I carefully bent my head to the door and sneaked a peak through the gap.

I could only really see part of Paul's back. He was sitting in front of the computer and I could see his hand pumping furiously at his lap. Leaving him to expel some of his desires, and hoping he wouldn't still be interested in me afterward, I tiptoed downstairs and made some chamomile tea.

At around that time, I was starting to see some light at the end of the tunnel. I had tens of thousands of dollars stashed away in an account under my own name. I was so close to being able to finally leave Paul that I'd begun looking at houses and apartments online. I'd estimated I needed to work for another month, maybe two in order to be completely settled financially. Then, I would be able to start looking for a 'regular' job; one that I could work part time. However, I had also considered the possibility of going back to school. If I got a degree, I'd be able to get a much better paying 'regular' job. I didn't yet know what subject I'd study, but it was an idea I was becoming fonder and fonder of.

With some rough calculations, that meant maybe another six months escorting and living under Paul's roof. Still, by summer of the following year, I would be free and in a much better position to get my life on track – with enough money to pay a mortgage and bills for a couple of years, and cover the cost of college tuition.

The positive news was that I now had four regular clients: submissive Steven, who was always a lot of fun; Marty, who was in his early fifties and always wanted to talk for three hours and then fuck for five minutes, which suited me fine; Tom, a young man who had the stamina of a marathon runner; and Damon, who had been in a motorcycle accident and was confined to a wheelchair. Damon had been told that his spinal injury wouldn't allow him to ever experience sexual sensations. However, the doctors were wrong – and he lapped up every single moment of that pleasure with a fervor I'd never seen in any other man.

And then, of course, there were the one-offs; the men who were drifting through the state on business. All told, I was working at least one night per week; sometimes two and, at very busy times, I'd have three dates in a week. When Paul was around, it was easy to claim I was heading out to a late night gym class. The now odd times he was spending away, I'd take the kids to their grandparents (my folks or Paul's), or arrange a sleepover at friends. When I was really stuck, or didn't want to incite the suspicion of Paul's Mom, I called on Becky, the babysitter I'd used for years.

Life was busy, it was active and I was enjoying it. So it's no great surprise that time flew. I was getting confident and comfortable, so much so that I had begun to feel like nothing could go wrong. That was my first mistake.

Chapter Seven
Line In The Sand

Scott was in his early to mid-thirties. He didn't tell me what he did for a living, but said he was passing through a town ten miles away from my home on a business trip. He asked if I could offer my services for a couple of hours on the Saturday night. I replied to his email, telling him I didn't usually offer such short dates – most of my clients requested four hours or more, many of them wanting to do something other than just have sex; even if it was just share an hour's conversation. He responded by asking how much I charged. I gave him the figure and was surprised when he said he'd pay me for four hours, but would only actually need me for two.

This seemed a little odd, but I'd met some pretty eccentric men who were quite carefree with their money. So, I didn't think too much of it and accepted his proposition.

The hotel he was staying in was very nice. A huge lobby with domed ceiling led to a wide, curving staircase. They'd maintained much of the style and décor of the 1920s, with lots of rounded edges. Even the corners of walls along the corridors were smoothly curved.

Scott was all the way up on the ninth floor, the building's highest and most expensive. This was where the suites were, all with panoramic views of the city below.

I knocked lightly on his door and within seconds was met by a pair of piercing blue eyes. He had a round face, with an angular jawline and trendily scruffy stubble. His light brown hair was short and spiky with neat sideburns that came down to his earlobes.

"Hey," he slurred, his cheeks reddened and eyes wavering. "Arianna, I assume," he added with a smirk. Flinging the door open wide, he stepped back.

"You assume correctly," I nodded, smiling at him as I entered the suite.

It was a large and luxurious space, an open plan living area and kitchen stretched out across the whole of the floor. Directly in front, were huge windows that spanned the entire length of one wall. These were covered by vertical blinds of a deep burgundy color. Glancing up, I noticed there was a mezzanine. I could only see the balcony of the upper floor, but assumed the bedroom would be found there.

A huge couch that could easily have seated six faced a fireplace and the huge television that hung on the wall. The floors were hardwood, but a white sheepskin rug was laid out in front of the couch. The kitchen, on the other hand, was a mixture of mahogany and stainless steel fittings. I guessed it didn't get much use – I assumed Scott hadn't even set foot in that direction.

"This is very nice," I commented, as my eyes finished their circuit of the room and settled once again on him.

As he rocked on the balls of his feet, he swayed. It was just a slightly uncoordinated motion, but it, along with his eyes and reddish complexion, left me with no doubt that he'd consumed his fair share of alcohol before I arrived. If it hadn't been for that, he would have appeared nicely put together. He was wearing a dark gray pair of dress pants with carefully pressed seams. On his upper half, he wore a white silk shirt, with silver cufflinks that had some kind of crest embossed on the face.

"Take your clothes off," he said, a smirk tugging at the corners of his mouth as his bright, blue eyes moved up and down the length of my short, black dress.

"Perhaps we ought to get the payment out of the way first," I suggested. Most of the men I'd met offered to pay upfront; were either familiar with the process or simply wanted to get the 'transaction' out of the way. A few that hadn't, I trusted to dig into their wallets after the date was over. Something about Scott, perhaps the fact he was drunk, made me wonder whether I'd have trouble getting the cash from him after he'd got what he wanted.

He didn't say anything as he slipped his right hand into his pocket and brought out a clutch of folded bills held together with a thin, gold money clip. With a flick of his hand, he tossed it towards me. The cash landed with a clink as the clip hit the hardwood, it skittered a few inches, stopping about a foot from me.

I looked questioningly at him, but when he still refused to speak, I slowly bent down. Keeping my knees together, I carefully reached for the money and scooped it from the floor. Giving a quick flick of the edges, I counted the bills and discovered that it was all there. Straightening, I removed the clip and opened my purse. After slipping the bills safely into my bag and snapping the catch shut, I held up his clip in the finger and thumb of my left hand.

He didn't seem interested. "Now, take your clothes off," he repeated, his feet unmoving and his face still appraising me.

Smiling at him, I took a couple of steps to my right. I kept my eyes on him, as I placed my purse and his money clip on the couch. My little black number had a plunging back and neckline. Slowly, I brought my right hand to my left shoulder and began to peel the strap away. I let it sink down my arm and the fabric of the dress at my chest almost immediately went slack. I used my right hand to keep it up, trying to reveal myself slowly and sexily to him. Once the other strap was slid from my shoulder, I released my hold on the top half of the dress and let it pool at my waist.

As could be expected, his gaze immediately moved to my breasts; the creamy globes of flesh and pink areolas. "Get it off," he insisted impatiently.

Without argument, I complied, taking hold of the fabric at my waist and carefully pushing it down. I gradually moved my hips in a slinky movement, as I smoothed the dress to my thighs and let it drop to the floor. Casually, I lifted one foot out of the circle of material then hooked the toes of my opposite foot into the dress and kicked it a couple of feet across the hardwood.

Clara James

I stood in nothing but my black, open-toed high heels; a pair of black hold ups, with three inches of patterned lace at the tops; and a black thong with a tiny, sheer triangle all that covered my sex.

His cheeks seemed to have become even more flushed, and he was eagerly swiping at his lower lip with his tongue. "Yeah," he muttered. "Yeah, you'll do."

"Thanks," I offered, smiling sweetly.

I expected him to come over to me, but instead his hand quickly delved into his other pocket. It emerged with a small transparent plastic bag that contained white powder. He quickly spun on one foot, moving rapidly to the kitchen. I remained still, simply watching him as he poured the powder onto one of the stainless steel counters. He then slipped a hand into his back pocket, grabbing his wallet. From that he grasped a credit card, which he used to split the lump of powder into two four inch lines.

"Come here," he beckoned, as he brought the edge of the credit card to his mouth and licked the freshly whitened edge.

"Not for me, thanks," I politely declined. I'd once been hired by a man who wanted to smoke marijuana before we had sex. It seemed to make him terribly drowsy, and the passive inhaling made me a little giggly. I'm not sure what it was doing for his sexual experience, but the only thing it did for me was make me terribly relaxed. In any case, until that point, that had been my only encounter with drugs. Cocaine was something else entirely and I knew enough about it to know that it was stupid to start taking it, even if it might make me feel like a million bucks for a couple of hours.

"This is good stuff," he said indignantly, as if he were offended.

"I'm sure it is," I quickly assured him with a smile. "But I don't take it."

He scoffed and tossed his credit card onto the counter. Taking a couple of steps toward me, he regarded me closely, his eyes dissecting me. "All of you whores love it," he stated. "That's what gets you through the night, huh?"

"I'm not a whore," I calmly replied. "And I don't need anything to get me through the night."

Half of his face drifted up in an unpleasant smile. "Don't kid yourself, babe," he chuckled. "You're a whore."

Technically, he might have been right. But, to me, the job of an escort was so much more than just sex. It was quickly becoming apparent that sex was all Scott wanted from me. He'd probably chosen me over an ordinary hooker for two reasons. First, a high class escort wouldn't look so out of place walking into a fancy place like that. And second, he assumed that, unlike a hooker, I was more selective over my clients and the protection I used. Of course, he was right.

"You're a filthy whore," he continued, the volume of his voice lowering as he took another step toward me. He was very close, so close he could have touched me. But he didn't. Instead, he continued to keep his hands casually in his pockets. "A dirty slut, who's had more dicks in her cunt than she can count."

As his face came closer to mine, I could see that the whites of his sparkling blue eyes were bloodshot. He was wrong, I knew exactly how many men I'd been with – remembered all their names and faces. I didn't bother to argue, though. He appeared to want me to be a 'whore', and he was paying far too much to quibble over a few words, no matter how vile. It was role-play, not vastly different from what I'd done many times with Steven. So, I stood calmly, quietly and accepted another barrage of filth from his mouth.

"How about your ass, huh? How many cocks have been up there? You're a slut; a useless piece of shit who's only good for fucking." He was growing angry as he spoke, with flecks of spittle being propelled from his lips. "A human sex toy," he added furiously. "That's all you are, bitch. So, don't fool yourself into thinking you're anything else."

The Escort Next Door

I swallowed, becoming nervous as his rage continued to amplify. Without warning, his hand snapped up from his pocket and gripped my face. I sucked in a surprised gasp, as his thumb dug angrily into one cheek. His fingers claimed the other and he squeezed hard, causing my lips to purse.

"Now," he said, his voice suddenly faux sweetness, in direct contrast to the grasp of his hand. "I'm going to have a line of coke and you're going to join me."

"I...Mmm...Ugh," I tried to speak, but my words were muffled from the position of my lips.

He shook his head, a sickly smile on his lips. "You don't seem to understand," he said, putting a little extra force into his fingers. "You're mine. I paid for you, and you'll do whatever the fuck I want." With his free hand, he grasped a tight hold of my wrist. He tugged me sharply towards the kitchen counter.

I didn't fight against him. However, my feet stumbled, one catching on the corner of the couch and causing me to stagger in order to stay upright.

When he got me where he wanted me, he quickly moved both of his hands. Snatching my waist, he pushed me forward, until my abdomen struck the edge of the counter.

"Hey," I mumbled. "If you want to play a bit rough, that's fine but-"

"Shut up, bitch!"

As it dawned on me that he was a little too involved in his fantasy, I quickly tried to regain control of the situation. "Listen," I said, fidgeting as I tried to wriggle out of his grasp.

"No," he sharply demanded, pushing himself against me and trapping me between his body and the kitchen counter. When he was sure I was secure, he took his right hand from my hip and grasped a fistful of my hair. "You listen. You're going to snort that line, because I want you to."

"Argh," I cried out, as he twisted his hand, until his knuckles were tight to my scalp.

With complete control of me, he pushed my face down to the counter. "Sniff it all up," he ordered. "Go on."

Using my hands to push against the counter had proven useless, so I began reaching behind me and trying to get a grip of him. It was futile, the light grasp I managed to make on his belt loops was not enough to gain any purchase against him.

"Snort it, you dirty, fucking whore," he shouted, pushing my face until my nose was crushed up on the counter.

"Argh," I cried out in pain. "All right," I wailed desperately. "All right."

The Escort Next Door

Gradually, he began to slacken his grip, but he kept his fingers wound in a long fistful of my hair.

I didn't really know what I was doing. However, I'd seen a few coke-snorting scenes in movies. So, crossing my fingers that the real thing was as portrayed, I drew my face down to the start of one of the lines. Using the forefinger of my right hand, I pressed against one nostril, and began to quickly inhale through the other. As I rapidly sucked up the powder, I moved down the line. It hurt like hell, a stabbing pain filling my sinuses almost immediately.

Once it was all gone, I lifted my head far too quickly and choked as some of the powder struck the back of my throat.

Scott was laughing and, as he released me, he quickly stepped back.

Suddenly lightheaded, I staggered backward and without him to stop me, I tripped over my own heels and landed with a loud clump on my butt. As I sat there, dazed and confused, I watched him take a fifty dollar bill from his pocket and roll it into a narrow cylinder. He then bent over the remaining line, taking half up one nostril, before switching for the other half. When he righted himself, he shook his head and drew the back of his hand over his nose.

As the seconds past and I glanced around the room, the world was becoming sharper. However, my heart was also pounding faster and harder in my chest; the rhythm something uneven and strained, as if it were about to stop at any moment.

Scott, on the other hand, was breathing deeply. His face turned up to the ceiling, while his eyes grew wider and something I couldn't identify filled them.

CHAPTER EIGHT
TIME TO RETIRE

I can't say whether my reactions were dulled or if his were heightened, a little of both perhaps, but as he suddenly rushed forward and grasped me beneath my arms it was with a speed that seemed to defy normal human ability. He pulled me to my feet with little effort and began dragging me, my useless feet refusing to work properly, toward the large windows at the end of the room.

As we reached the panoramic windows, he must have grabbed the cord for the blinds, because the next thing I knew I was being shoved face-first into bare glass. My breasts were squashed against the cold surface, as I panted hard. The lights from buildings and traffic below were blindingly bright, made even more painful by a shooting pain that was pulsing up my left temple. Everything, including his voice, seemed so much more powerful than before.

"I think we should let all the people down there know what a filthy whore you are, don't you?"

I couldn't answer, my brain was whirring too quickly; trying to take in every detail, even minute ones like the flickering of a TV set across the street.

"Now everybody knows. The whole world knows what you are." As he talked, he slowly pressed himself against the length of my back and I began to realize just how turned on he was. The solid tip of his erection was poking at the top of my right buttock and it, like everything else I could see, hear and feel, seemed larger than life. "They know you're nothing. They know you're a worthless slut."

He coaxed another gasp of surprise from me, when he suddenly pulled back and tugged me with him. "Wha...?" I tried to incoherently question, as he guided me ten feet from the window and thrust me toward the back of the couch. My lower abdomen hit the hard wood at the top of the furniture. And, with the flat of his palm on the top of my spine, he shoved me until my head was almost touching the seat cushions.

By that point, my hair was covering my face. All I could see was the fabric of the couch, between curtains of long brunette strands. "Ugh," I mumbled, as I heaved for oxygen that there didn't seem to be enough of. "Con..." I muttered, feebly. "Condom."

He was viciously pulling my underwear down when he laughed humorlessly. "You think I'd put my dick in that disgusting, hand-me-down cunt without protection?" he spat. "You couldn't pay *me* for that, bitch."

I don't know how much time passed; things seemed to be happening in fast forward. My memory of what occurred next is blurry, and I suppose that's something I should be grateful for, because the hazy things I do remember I wish I didn't.

He entered me roughly, spearing my sex with a savage thrust that pushed me further over the couch. He didn't pause for breath. Instead, he instantly began pumping his hips viciously against my buttocks.

As the blood rushing to my head causing my vision to darken, I whimpered and muttered words of pain and discomfort. But this just seemed to spur him on. He wanted to hurt me; got a kick out of his position of power and the ability to inflict pain. With one hand at the nape of my neck, he kept my face pinned to the couch, while the other reached around my chest and brutally gripped one of my breasts.

"How do you like that, you dirty, fucking bitch?" Each of his shouted, angry words was punctuated by a hurried, violent thrust that buried his rigid shaft deep within me. "Filthy whore!" he added, squeezing my breast in his strong hand. "This is all you're good for." He growled as he rammed harder and harder, seeming to want to cut me in two. "Ugh, you cunt!"

I'm fairly sure I made no more than plaintive, whispered moans and cries in reply. It was all I could muster. The roof of my mouth pulsed with the hammer of my heart; blood was rushing like massive waves against my eardrums. And then, everything went black.

I would say that I'd passed out, but I know that can't have been the case. At least, I couldn't have stayed passed out, because the next thing I was aware of was waking up in my own bed. So, somehow I must have left the hotel, made my way home and managed to find the bed. I was naked beneath the sheet, with my dress discarded on the floor. Next to it was my purse, which, I would later discover, still contained the $10,000 Scott had paid me.

Fortunately, Paul was away that weekend; he'd gone on a golfing trip with one of his cousins. I'd left the children with Fran, a woman from the school, whose daughter was good friends with Lizzie. She also had a son who was just a bit older than Dylan. That didn't leave Kate with a playmate, but Fran was baby-hungry and more than happy to have a two-year-old running around the house again.

It's only with retrospect that I've been able to appreciate these things. At the time, all I was aware of was the pounding of my head and the ache that raked through every inch of my body. It felt a little like a bad bout of flu. I don't know whether it was the after effects of the coke, or if Scott gave me something else over the course of the evening – the latter was certainly possible.

In any case, as I strained my neck to read the clock, I realized it was close to midday – an hour after I was supposed to have picked up the kids. I tired, but couldn't lift myself quickly. Instead, it was a steady shuffling into a seated position. As soon as I was upright, I could see the phone and the blinking light of the answering machine. Not bothering to listen to the message, I leaned for the phone and tapped in the numbers for Fran's home.

"Hello?" she answered after the fourth ring.

"Hi," I said, my voice hoarse and gravelly. "Fran," I added, trying to clear my throat. "It's me, Julia."

"Oh, hey," she responded. "We were getting worried. Are you okay?"

"I...umm," I mumbled, my throat dray and scratchy. "I'm not feeling great," I added, in a masterpiece of understatement.

"Oh, no," she said sympathetically. "You don't sound too good, honey. Are you coming down with something?"

"Uhhh, maybe," I muttered. "Could you do me a huge favor and watch the kids for another couple of hours. I'm going to try to get myself together."

"Well, sure," she responded quickly. "If you need me to watch them longer than that, I can. I've got to go to work at six, but until then-"

"It's fine," I softly told her, ending her need to finish the sentence. "Thank you," I quickly added, realizing I sounded ungrateful. "I think I'll be okay. I'll try to be there in two hours."

"Okay," she said. "And it's no problem. Oh, and make sure to drink plenty of water," she advised warmly.

"Yeah, I will," I nodded, cursing the movement of my head when it caused pain to bolt through every nerve in my skull. "Thanks again, Fran." I didn't wait for her reply. I couldn't wait. Quickly, I jabbed a button to end the call and tossed the phone aside on the mattress. Getting out from under the sheets as fast as possible, I made my way ungainly toward the bathroom; grabbing hold of everything that could steady me along the way. I didn't manage to make it to the toilet, but I was close enough to the tub, and that's where I threw up.

Afterward, I collapsed onto the bathmat and laid flat on my back for several minutes. I didn't go to sleep. Didn't even close my eyes. I just watched the slow spinning of the ceiling, willing it to cease.

Eventually, I don't know how long it took; the world did seem to find an equilibrium once more. Things were still mushy to my eyes and ears, but at least I could sit and stand without feeling seasick. Being as gentle as possible with myself, I took a nice long shower.

It was then that I began to realize exactly how violent Scott had been the night before. I had raw bruises on my upper arms and wrists; an angry red hand print on my left breast; marks on my inner thighs, which suggested the encounter had involved more penetration than I remembered; and, when I got out of the shower and caught sight of myself in the mirror, I noticed discoloration beneath my left eye and a small cut to my lower lip.

I couldn't be sure when the injuries to my face occurred. I guessed it was when Scott pushed me into the thick plate glass window. However, knowing that there was much more about the night I didn't remember, I couldn't disregard the possibility that he'd knocked me around.

The entire area between my thighs was tender and when I went to pee, my internal muscles complained strongly about the way my channel had been abused.

But it was much more than just the physical aftermath of what happened. It was what was going on in my head that really hurt – the foul names he'd called me; the sense that he was right, I am worthless. And the question kept rolling around, 'How could I have been so stupid?' I'd known what I was getting into was dangerous, and yet the positive encounters I'd had until that night lulled me into a false sense of security. I'd begun to think I was invincible, that nothing bad could happen to me. These men were paying large sums of money to sleep with me, they couldn't possibly be thugs. Idiot.

As I made my way back to the bedroom, wrapped in a thick terry cloth robe, I knew that it was over. The big dreams I'd had were not going to be fulfilled, because there was no way I'd put myself through that again – I couldn't. I would have to take another look at the money I'd saved and forge a plan with that. It would mean college was an impossibility for now. Nevertheless, there were more important things. If I could get an apartment or small home for the children, that was what mattered. The rest, I'd have to play by ear.

The Escort Next Door

I put a thick layer of make-up on and wore a pair of sunglasses when I went to pick up the kids. Despite my best efforts, Fran noted that I appeared very pale. I attributed this to me not being well. And, as it happened, she had no trouble believing that I'd fallen while suffering from a fever, which explained my cut lip. It seemed that the terrible secret of what really happened would remain with me.

When Paul returned the next day, he didn't even notice. By then, I was feeling better, although the bruises were quickly turning purple and blue, and some color was returning to my complexion. For the next week, I was sure to wear a high-necked shirt and avoid Paul unless I was fully dressed, because the big fingermarks that crept out of the edge of my bra could not be so easily explained by a bout of the flu.

Another week and the marks began to fade. My memories of that night still haunted me, though. I felt used, dirty and worthless; all the things he'd said I was. And it didn't help, of course, that my own husband avoided touching me like the plague.

For twelve days, I avoided the computer and my cell phone. My regular clients had my number and would occasionally send a subtle, discrete text rather than an email. I didn't want to hear from any of them. Even those I'd been with before, men I had trusted – I couldn't bear the thought of having anyone inside me. On the thirteenth day, however, I realized I couldn't just disappear. I'd have to contact my regulars and let them know I was retiring from the business.

And that's exactly what I planned to do when I sat down at the computer late one Friday night, while Paul was in his office on a conference call with clients in Australia.

I had twenty unread messages. I began checking the little box to the left of each in turn, planning to delete them all in one fell swoop. I can't explain what caused me to pause, but when I reached an email with the subject line, 'Looking for a companion for formal dinner' I stopped in my tracks. It was ridiculous, the fact that this man was attending a fancy dinner told me nothing about his attitude towards women or sex. And yet, somehow I was intrigued.

It was not the first time since I found out about Paul's infidelities that I'd acted completely without logical thought or planning. But it was probably the occasion that shocked me most. Every fiber in my being was screaming at me to severe all contacts and get the hell out of the business. Yet, I was opening this email and reading with interest.

Arianna,

I've read your ad and I was wondering if you're available next Saturday. I'm attending a function at the Hilton and *would love it if you could accompany me. I know it's very short notice, and, I should warn you, it'll be quite a long night – I'll need you to meet me at 7 and the dinner probably won't be over until after midnight. So, I'm willing to compensate you. How does $25,000 sound? If this is less than your usual rate, let me know and I'll be happy to negotiate.*

It was signed 'Preston' and, next to his name, he included a cell phone number. If I'd been able to think rationally, I would have deleted the email and forgotten all about it. However, I wasn't thinking at all. I was acting on impulse – focusing on the $25,000 I could earn with just one night's work. Except I don't think I was even considering that. I wasn't weighing up the reward and risks. Something was just compelling me to call him.

And so I did. Right then and there; at eleven o'clock at night, I dialed his number.

"Hello?" he muttered groggily. His voice was deep, a baritone that was warm and rumbling.

"I'm sorry," I quickly apologized. "Did I wake you?"

"Umm," he hummed, pausing while he seemed to get his bearings. "Uhh, yeah," he eventually agreed. "I guess you did, but it's okay. What can I do for you?"

"Well," I hesitated, suddenly nervous. Was it that the reality of what I was doing had hit me? Was I having second thoughts? I don't know, but as I held the phone to my ear, it trembled with the persistent shaking of my fingers. "Actually, it's about what I can do for you," I managed to softly announce.

"Huh?" he asked, bewildered.

"My name's Arianna," I told him, aware that the tremble was now starting to creep into my voice.

"Ohhh," he breathed, the realization striking him quickly. "Oh," he repeated. "Thanks so much for calling. I'm really glad to hear from you."

"My pleasure," I responded, attempting to fake a sultry confidence. "So, what can I do for you, Preston?" I added saucily.

CHAPTER NINE
BELLE OF THE BALL

Preston was perfectly polite and gentlemanly on the phone, which gave me the courage to get ready and leave the house the following Saturday night. However, in the cab on the way to the address he'd given me, I was beginning to have second thoughts. Flashes of Scott's face, his angry words and violent grasp filled my thoughts completely. Twice, I almost told the driver to turn around, convinced that I couldn't put myself through it again. But something was still keeping me from running away. To this day, I don't know what it was. At the time, all I could do was hope that, whatever it was, it wasn't leading me down another dark and scary path.

The car pulled to a stop outside an apartment building. "This is you," the driver announced.

"Thanks," I acknowledging, leaning forward to pay him before reaching for the door. I slowly shuffled out of the car, keeping one hand on the long hem of my floor-length midnight blue gown. It was brand new. I had plenty of dresses that would have been acceptable for a formal occasion, but, for reasons unknown to me, none of them felt right. My hair was neatly styled in an up do, with two wavy strands falling either side of my face. I was wearing a diamond necklace that my parents had bought me for my wedding day and matching droplet earrings which I'd purchased for myself on our first anniversary.

The ground floor of the apartment building was all glass and with the bright lights of the lobby gleaming, it was possible to see inside. All that was in the spacious area was a corner desk with a man in his early sixties sitting behind it. He had a computer in front of him, but he was reading a newspaper that was spread out next to the keyboard.

Carefully, I made my way to the door and found it pushed easily open. The smooth sound alerted the security guard, he looked up from his crossword puzzle and smiled at me.

"Good evening, Miss," he greeted with a nod. "Can I help you?"

My heels clipped loudly on the marble floors and echoed in the otherwise soundless space. "Umm, I'm here to see Preston Verrill."

"Oh, of course," he nodded, flipping the paper closed and picking up a phone that was hidden beneath the pages. "Mr. Verrill said he was expecting a young lady. One moment." As he spoke he picked up the phone and tapped three digits into the pad. He smiled at me, while waiting for a response on the other end. "Mr. Verrill, it's Hank downstairs," he said into the phone. "Yes," he then nodded. "All right, thank you."

Trying to give my right hand something to do, I fiddled with my necklace while I watched him replace the phone.

"He'll be down in a few moments; he asked if you could please wait."

"Of course," I replied nodding. I suppose by then I should have been feeling a little more relaxed. After all, Preston had given me his name, his home address and had obviously told his doorman that he was expecting me. None of those seemed like the actions of a psycho. But, of course, that didn't mean he couldn't be like Scott. However, it was far too late to change my mind.

It was less than a minute before the elevator doors gently swept open. My eyes began at his shoes, the highly polished black Oxfords, and moved up his perfectly pressed black tux with vest. Beneath that, he wore a crisp white shirt and a maroon bow tie. From his left breast pocket poked a neatly folded handkerchief that matched his tie's color.

As I gradually allowed my gaze to move higher, I was surprised by how young he appeared. His deep voice and his success in whatever it was he did for a living, had naturally caused me to picture someone older; a man well into his forties, maybe even fifty. However, Preston's fresh, clean shaven face put him at thirty five at the oldest. Looking back, I think it was his incredibly broad smile, which was genuine warmth and all dazzling, perfect white teeth that made him look youthful.

He had soft features, but his cheekbones were sharply defined and he had a strong jawline. He wore a pair of light-framed glasses over his dark brown eyes. His hair, which was a slighter lighter brown, was short at the back and side with just a little length at the top that enabled him to part it on one side and slick it over in a fashion reminiscent of the 1940s. "Hello, Arianna," he said warmly, with an easy smile. He walked toward me reaching out his right hand.

"Hello," I replied, swallowing the nerves that refused to leave me completely, and offering him my hand.

He took it in his, but not as though he intended to shake it. Instead, he wrapped his fingers around mine while he leaned forward and pressed his lips to my cheekbone. It was the left, the one that was still slightly bruised from my date with Scott, now a sickly yellow rather than blue, but I'd managed to cover the discoloration with concealer and felt certain that it wouldn't show. As I inhaled, a got a lungful of his clean scent; it was obvious he had not long since got out of the shower.

"Thanks so much for coming," he said, as he pulled back. "You look amazing. Sorry I don't have time to invite you up for a drink, but we really need to get going or we'll be late."

"That's okay," I softly replied, as he straightened and I noticed, even with my heels, I only came up to his chin.

"Great," he nodded. "Well, err," he added, releasing my hand, "this way."

I followed him, as he led me back the way I'd entered. He pushed the door open and held it, encouraging me to go first. I nodded gratefully as I passed him and tossed a quick glance behind me. There was the security guard, smiling back at me. I managed to offer him an uneasy grin, before forced to face forward and look where I was going.

As soon as I got onto the sidewalk, a black sedan limo drew to a halt in front of me. Preston's arm then reached out from behind me and guided me forward. Quietly, I watched as he opened the door and I slipped into the backseat when he gestured for me to do so.

It wasn't until he was sat beside me and the door was securely closed that he spoke again. "So, umm, just so you know what we're doing. This is a benefit dinner for homeless and underprivileged kids in the state. I'll do my best not to leave you alone, but if we do get separated, just be yourself."

"You're worried, I'll embarrass you?" I asked, turning my neck swiftly so I could face him.

"No," he replied, with an effortless chuckle. "Of course, not," he added. "You seem a little nervous, and I was just trying to reassure you that there's no need to be."

"I'm sorry," I rapidly muttered, shaking my head as I quickly removed me eyes from his face. "I didn't mean to..." My efforts to backtrack stalled and I shrugged uselessly.

"It's fine," he replied, dismissing it just as fast as I'd brought it up. He changed the subject, telling me a little about himself. He was a lawyer, but he seemed to brush over that as though he were ashamed of it.

He was thirty four and had always hated attending these functions alone.

The word 'always' implied that he hadn't had a lot of luck in relationships, but I wondered if I was reading too much into it.

"I've never hired an escort before," he admitted. "But, umm, well..." he paused, tipping his head to one side and looking out the window. After a second, he began to laugh self-deprecatingly. "I don't really know what made me look," he said. "But when I saw your ad, I had a feeling that you'd be perfect."

I didn't know how to respond to that, so I did the only thing I could; smiled politely and looked bashfully at my lap.

"So, tell me about yourself," he eventually said, shuffling around in his seat fractionally.

"Me?" I blurted.

"Yeah, you," he chuckled. "I want to know more about you."

Very few of the men I'd worked for wanted to know anything about me. The odd one or two that had, might have thought they did; but when I turned the topic of conversation back to them, they didn't hesitate to continue conversing about themselves.

And Preston certainly didn't want to know about me, either. Not the real me, anyway. "What sort of thing do you want to know?" I asked, with a half shrug.

"I don't know," he smiled. "Anything. What interests you?"

"Right now," I sighed, going into one of my well-used lines. "You're the only thing that interests me."

His smile turned skeptical and he cocked his head. "I mean it," he said, arching an eyebrow. "I don't just want to talk at you; I want us to have a conversation."

"We can have a conversation," I replied. "Pick a topic, politics? Music? Movies?"

"You," he insisted.

Sighing, I glanced at the roof of the car's interior, a large expanse of smooth gray. "Listen," I told him quietly. "I don't-"

"You don't want to," he supplied, with an understanding nod. "That's okay. I'm sorry, I shouldn't have pushed it."

"It's..." I breathed, faltering. "It's a little more complicated than that," I offered, not wanting to hurt his feelings by letting him assume that he was just another client and, therefore, I didn't want to let him get to close. Of course, there was an element of that – no question. But it was much more complex. "Men who hire women like me, are buying more than just an evening with a person." As I tried to put the thoughts racing through my head into coherent sentences, I stared at my hands entwined in my lap. "They're buying a fantasy. Who I am, what I am; it's all in their heads. I just become whatever it is they want."

He looked at me pensively, digesting that. "I'm sure that's the case a lot of times," he nodded. "But what if what I want is you. Just you," he added for emphasis.

"You don't know that," I good-naturedly argued, flashing him a sideways glance.

"That's true," he conceded, smiling. "But neither of us will ever know if I don't get to know the real you."

I never replied; didn't exactly know how. The truth was I didn't know who the real me was any more. I was no longer the wife I thought I'd been, wasn't the good girl who had only ever slept with one man. I didn't have anything beyond a high school education; I wasn't employed in a worthwhile job. Maybe Scott was right. I was nothing, except a warm hole for men to fill. The real me was nothing, no one, a whore.

I don't know if I looked troubled by my thoughts, but Preston didn't push the subject any further. Instead, he chatted about inane things throughout the rest of the journey. I joined in when I could – a nod here, a 'yes' there or something more if I felt able to contribute an opinion. But it was all done on autopilot.

When we arrived at the Hilton, Preston offered me his hand and helped me out of the car. He then placed his palm at the small of my back, which I felt sure was just to guide me into the hotels massive ballroom. However, his fingers moved in gentle circles, seeming to silently reassure and comfort me.

He introduced me to a handful of people, offered me some champagne and I stood in a loose circle with him and five others, as they talked about the charity and its aims.

"I definitely think we need to do more," Preston insisted passionately. "It's not enough just to give them hot meals for a few weeks and expect them to be able to get on their own feet. They need the support to get them back into school or into work if necessary."

"How do you propose we do that?" a silver-haired man asked.

"Education," Preston replied simply. "We teach them the skills they need, basic reading and writing – whatever it is that's preventing them from being able to get off the streets."

"Most of them are on drugs, Preston," a silver-haired woman, presumably the man's wife, commented sharply. "They don't want to better themselves, they want to get their next hit."

"Or maybe they want their next hit, because their lives are so awful they feel that's all they have," I offered, not thinking before I spoke. For a second, I stood with my mouth hanging open, wondering whether I should take it back and swinging a panicked look in the direction of my date.

He didn't look concerned. In fact, he looked pleased, he was positively beaming.

"Well," the woman mumbled grudgingly. "Well, perhaps," she admitted. "But I still say we need to get them clean before we can do anything else."

"Perhaps," I offered, with a quirk of my head. "And perhaps, while we stand here swigging fancy, French champagne, we have no right to judge."

"Amen," Preston instantly blurted. "There but for the grace of God, right Mrs. Campbell?"

The woman looked as though she'd just been slapped round the face. Everybody else in the group was silent. I noticed a couple of them smiling, but the others looked just as scandalized as Mr. and Mrs. Campbell.

"Now, if you'll excuse us," Preston announced, placing his champagne on a passing waiter's tray. "We're going to take a spin on the dance floor." He took my glass from me, and handed it to a man whose name I don't think I was ever told. Then, he carefully offered me his hand and led me away from the group, some of whom stared daggers at us.

When we found a pocket of space on the dance floor, close to the band, he wrapped an arm around my back and pulled me close. He raised his other hand, which clutched mine, to the height of his shoulder. "Do you dance?" he whispered hurriedly.

"Yes," I giggled in return. "I can dance."

"Good," he grinned, as he began to slowly sway in time with the music.

Little was spoken while we danced, but we shared smiles. And before I knew it, I was becoming quite intoxicated by the feeling of his body against mine. We seemed to fit together, in a way I'd never experienced dancing with anyone else. Every movement was in sync, no stubbing of toes against the others, no awkward banging of hip bones. It was all smooth and effortless. It was becoming easier for me to forget what had happened with Scott. It was even becoming possible for me to look forward to what would happen when we got back to Preston's apartment. Perhaps it was foolishness on my part; an assumption that any adolescent girl would be proud of, but it seemed to me that if our bodies moved so well together while upright, he would be equally sensual and tender when it came to the bedroom.

Chapter Ten
Captivated

I was sad when Preston suggested we take a break and leave the dance floor, but tried not to show it and smiled as he took my hand. While we were heading to the bar, we were stopped by a photographer. With my hand reassuringly tucked in his, I leaned into him as a couple of shots were quickly snapped. That was my second mistake.

Unfortunately, it was several more hours before we could leave. There were a couple of auctions and several speeches that had to be sat through. Eventually, at around twelve thirty, the room began to empty.

"Are you ready to leave?" Preston asked, getting up and unbuttoning his jacket.

"Sure," I nodded, lifting myself out of my seat.

"Okay," he said tipping his head towards the entrance and offering me his arm.

Clara James

Without needing to be asked twice, I reached out and looped my hand through his arm. And without realizing I was doing it, I nestled closely to him as we wandered from the ballroom, across the lobby and out the revolving front door.

The limo was once again waiting and we were able to quickly slip inside. When we'd pulled away from the hotel, Preston slid his hand into his inside jacket pocket and pulled out his wallet. He rummaged through a stack of cash before pulling it from its leather sleeve and handing it to me. "I meant to give you this earlier," he said with a smile. "Sorry about that."

"No, it's fine," I responded, accepting the money and quickly tucking it into my purse. I didn't count it, didn't spend any time lingering over how thick it felt and how incredible it was that I'd been paid so much for an evening's work, because I didn't want to think about being paid for 'work'. The night had been great. Even the boring parts of the evening, had been made fun simply by being with him. He was kind, sharp-witted, intelligent and generous. I'd been able to forget everything: my horrible experience with Scott and Paul's affairs. Not to mention, the fact that I was with Preston because I was being paid to be. The stark reminder that it was, indeed, about money made me very uncomfortable.

The Escort Next Door

"You were incredible tonight," he said, his hand lying casually on my knee. "I had a lot of fun."

"Me too," I responded, feeling the need to cover his fingers and keep them on my leg. The warmth of them was easily seeping through the thin fabric of my dress and I enjoyed the sensation. I needed to be touched like that; a gentle, affectionate touch. It was what I'd been craving for far too long.

He glanced at my fingers, entwining with his and keeping them captive, then looked back at my face. "I have a feeling that I saw glimpses of the real you tonight," he commented smoothly. "I hope so," he added, "because I like her."

I reluctantly gave him a half-smile, but refused to be drawn further into that discussion. As far as I was concerned, it was still my job to be what he wanted me to be. If he wouldn't outright tell me what that was, I'd have to figure it out on the fly. But figure it out I would, because being myself was not part of the gig. Never had been, not even the very first time, although admittedly there had been more of 'me' in the woman who had sex with my first client.

"Do you go to those sorts of things often?" I asked, very deliberately changing the subject.

He leaned back in the seat, causing his hand to move a little with him. Thankfully, it didn't lift from my leg, but it crept from my knee up to my thigh.

"Not very many," he shrugged. "I always help the needy when I can, and they tell me those sorts of things raise a lot of money, but I can't stand being around all those snobs."

"Yeah," I responded thoughtfully, as I studied his face. "They don't really seem like your crowd."

"Hmm," he chuckled, with a tired nod. "I enjoyed this one, though. Thank you for coming with me."

"Thank you for inviting me," I responded quietly.

The atmosphere in the back of the car was beginning to change, it was becoming more intimate and I wondered for a moment whether he was going to kiss me. However, he didn't move. Instead, he continued to look at my face, smiling amiably.

Our drive back to his apartment building was quicker, the traffic was much lighter I suppose. Either that, or I was that much more comfortable on the return journey. In any case, the car was soon drawing to a halt.

I expected Preston to grab the door and immediately jump out. After waiting all night, he must have been aching to get me upstairs. However, he didn't move. For what felt like an eternity, he just sat there. "Listen, I...umm..." he eventually mumbled, his eyes drifting to his hand on my mid-thigh. "I wanna say thanks again."

It crossed my mind to say something smart like, 'Don't thank me yet!' but I remained quiet. It was clear he hadn't finished what he wanted to say.

The leather seat squeaked as he shuffled forward and kissed me once more on the cheekbone. It was as tender and pure as the first. As he pulled away, he used his free hand to stroke the spot his lips had just touched. "You're really something special," he whispered, his dark eyes locked onto mine as he spoke.

Grinning shyly, I felt heat flush my cheeks.

"Goodnight, Arianna," he whispered.

"Goodnight?" I queried, confusion creasing my brow.

"Thanks for a wonderful evening," he nodded, slipping his hand gracefully out from beneath mine.

"But," I mumbled. "I thought..." I stopped when I realized I didn't have a tactful way to say it.

"It's late," he offered kindly, with one of his brightest, widest smiles. "I think maybe we better call it a night."

"Are you sure?" I gabbled. "I mean, I thought you paid for..." Again, I didn't finish the sentence, I just left it hanging there. I'd yet to be hired by any man that didn't want to have sex in some shape or form at some point during the evening. I certainly hadn't been offered the kind of money Preston had just given me to simply hang on someone's arm all night.

"I paid for the pleasure of your company," he told me simply. "And that's exactly what I got."

I tried to wrap my head around what was happening, as he smiled once more and began to pull open the door handle.

"Let Darren know where you want to go," Preston said, as he lifted himself from the seat and turned back to face me. Bending, he leaned his upper half through the open doorway. "I've asked him to make sure you get home safely."

I hadn't known the driver's name was Darren, but the context left no other explanation. "I'm fine," I quickly assured him. "I'll get a cab. I don't want to put Darren through the trouble."

"It's no trouble," Preston insisted, the finger and thumb of one hand adjusting his glasses.

For several seconds, I stared at him; his genuine, honest, open face and the smile that he continued to lavish me with. He was like no other man I'd ever met. And I don't just mean like no other client I'd met. I mean, he was like no other man I'd known in my life. It was incredibly hard to fight the way I was drawn to him.

"Please," he urged, assuming I suppose that I was still grappling with whether to let his driver take me home. "I just want to know you get back okay."

"You know," I sighed, leaning forward and taking my turn to kiss him on the cheek. "You're something very special, Mr Verrill." I smiled at him as I sank slowly back into the seat. "I don't think they make 'em like you anymore."

With a lopsided grin, he cocked his head. "I'm not sure about that," he mumbled. "You take care," he added, suddenly righting himself and shutting the door with a heavy clunk.

During the drive back to my place, I was in a trance-like state, imagining what could have been if he'd invited me upstairs. He would never have just fucked me, of that I was certain. It wasn't in him. And God knows, if that's what he wanted, he could have had it. He could have had it before we even went to the function.

No, he would have taken his time. He would have caressed me, kissed me, and made love to me. The thought of it sent heat radiating throughout my body and I was forced to crack the window open.

However, those pleasant thoughts and that warm sensation began to leave me when I questioned what had happened. I was glad he didn't just want to use me for a quick screw. But it seemed he didn't want me at all.

Why?

Did my behavior during the evening turn him off? Was it simply the thought that I slept with men for money that gnawed away at him all night and then, ultimately, he couldn't go through with it? Did he think, like Scott, that I was just a worthless hand-me-down; a filthy whore?

No, that didn't make sense. If he thought of me as nothing, then why was he concerned about my safety, why had he kept grinning at me like that and why had he said unnecessarily sweet things? So, what was wrong with me?

I arrived home at just before two in the morning. I dashed to the shed in the yard, changing into some gym clothes, removing most of my makeup and taking my hair down, before entering the house. As it turned out, the charade was a waste of time, because Paul was fast asleep on the couch. He didn't rouse when I shut the front door, nor did he stir when I climbed the stairs.

Usually, when I'd been working, I'd have a shower as soon as I got back – even if I'd been able to have one before I'd left my client. That night, I wandered straight down the hall, opened each of the kids' bedroom doors in turn and wished them a quiet, hushed goodnight that they never heard.

I had everything I needed to go. I had enough money to get away from Paul and start a new life. I would never have to sell myself again; not to a stranger and not to my husband. I was finally free. I told myself this repeatedly, as I shuffled back to my bedroom and slowly peeled off my clothes. It didn't matter whether Preston wanted to sleep with me or not. In fact, it was good that he didn't. It meant I got paid, and didn't have to give away a part of myself that I'd never wanted to offer in the first place.

I got involved with the business, because I felt I had to. I'd then deluded myself into thinking that it was something I enjoyed – when the painful truth is I always knew that it was slowly eating away at my soul. Bit by bit and night by night, I was chipping away at my moral foundation; who I was and what I held dear. I only had to think about my two girls growing up and doing what I'd been doing to know that I was thoroughly disgusted by what I'd done.

Was I sorry? No. Did I regret it? No. It was worth the sacrifice.

What bothered me was that I couldn't stop thinking about Preston. It frustrated me that a part of my brain, a stupid vain part, wouldn't stop feeling rejected by the fact he'd chosen not to take me to bed. That part of me was starting to create an anger deep within, because the unruly voice went against everything else I believed in.

Clara James

Paul never came to bed. I never got any sleep. I slipped beneath the sheets, but stared at the ceiling, until the sun rose. When I wasn't thinking about Preston's kind, brown eyes, I was busy wondering how I was going to leave Paul. If I made a run for it, I'd lose the kids. If I told him I was leaving, he'd still fight me for the kids, but there was a good chance a fair judge would give me primary custody; after all Paul spent a third of his time jetting all over the country and even when he wasn't, he worked twelve hours a day.

Eventually, I decided that it would be better to buy a house, before I announced the news to Paul. That way, I'd be able to leave right away. As it stood, if I waltzed downstairs and told him I knew he put his dick in just about every woman he'd ever worked with, I still had nowhere to go – at least not immediately.

Technically, I might have been free. But there were still a few hoops to jump through, before it was truly a reality. While I was morosely contemplating that fact, I heard the buzz of my cell phone vibrating against the bedside table. Initially, I chose to ignore it. But every few seconds, the phone would remind me that I had an unread message, vibrating perpetually until the noise was driving me crazy.

"For Christ's sake," I muttered, flipping over onto my side and grabbing the phone angrily. I jabbed it roughly with my thumb and the text opened up on the screen.

'Arianna, at the risk of overstating it, just wanted to say I had a really good time last night. I was hoping that I'd be able to see you again. Same price. Any time. Let me know.'

In my sleep-deprived state, I had to read the message three times, before I was certain I understood it. Preston was willing to pay another $25,000 for an evening with me. I'd been wrong in assuming he didn't like me or was turned off by what I did for a living. That didn't, of course, explain the game he was playing.

I knew I should toss it aside, ignore it. I didn't need that money. Yes, it would be nice. It would have added to my financial security, but I didn't need it. However, yet again, a part of my brain was operating without the permission of the rest. My thumb was already typing out a reply.

'Preston, good to hear from you. I'd be delighted to see you again and the terms are fine. I'm free any night this week.'

At that time, I had no way of knowing whether or not what I'd just done was the worst decision of my life. It certainly could be. It would be some months, before I'd know for sure.

To Be Continued…

Also by bestselling author

Clara James

~The Escort Next Door Series~

The Escort Next Door

The Escort Next Door: Captivated

The Escort Next Door: Escape

~Her Last Love Affair Series~

Her Last Love Affair

Her Last Love Affair: Breathing Without You

Her Last Love Affair: The Final Journey

To view these titles visit:
http://amzn.to/15ek5q7

Printed in Great Britain
by Amazon